'Are we so in

'There's at least
wholly compatible

Lucia regarded him warily. 'I believe it's called lust,' she allowed sweetly.

'I believe it's called sexual attraction. It happened to me too, you know,' he added gently.

'That doesn't mean we have to do anything about it!'

She had no intention of exploring any physical attraction with a man who didn't respect her— and how could he when he was prepared to blackmail her?

Jayne Bauling was born in England and grew up in South Africa. She always wrote but was too shy to show anyone until the publication of some poems in her teens gave her the confidence to attempt the romances she wanted to concentrate on, the first published being written while she was attending business college. Her home is just outside Johannesburg, a town house ruled by a sealpoint called Ranee. Travel is a major passion; at home it's family, friends, music, swimming, reading and patio gardening.

Recent titles by the same author:

SOPHISTICATED SEDUCTION

SUBSTITUTE ENGAGEMENT

BY
JAYNE BAULING

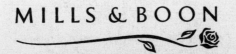

MILLS & BOON

*MILLS & BOON and the Rose Device
are trademarks of the publisher.
Harlequin Mills & Boon Limited,
Eton House, 18–24 Paradise Road, Richmond, Surrey TW9 1SR*

© Jayne Bauling 1996

ISBN 0 263 79521 7

*Set in 10 on 11 pt Linotron Times
01-9606-57707*

*Typeset in Great Britain by CentraCet, Cambridge
Made and printed in Great Britain*

CHAPTER ONE

SHE had kept her promise to her father. Now it was time to keep another—that given to Thierry Olivier, too long ago for her liking.

Lucia's sensitive mouth curved happily at the thought of the beautiful man she loved.

For the moment she couldn't spot his bright red-gold head anywhere among the crowd thronging the attractive open-air functions area of Grande Comore's newest hotel, one of the Ballard Group and the latest in a chain gracing most of the popular holiday islands of the Indian Ocean.

Thierry hadn't been at Hahaya Airport to meet her, of course. As this was early in November, flights from South Africa were not fully booked and she had managed to get on to one a week earlier than she had originally anticipated.

Nor had he been at home when the taxi had delivered her to the Olivier estate, but the new housekeeper there had told her that he and his mother were at the hotel, so she had set out to find them, hailing the first of the local taxis to pass—one of the fourteen-seater Peugeot trucks, or 'bakkies', as she had learnt to call them during her three years in South Africa.

Lucia had wondered a little at Thierry's absence from the estate at this hour on a Saturday afternoon, but when she'd failed to find him in the main bar the presence of several familiar faces among the gathering outdoors had seemed to suggest some local celebration for which this area had been hired.

But the face that distracted her gaze from its roving quest for Thierry was definitely unfamiliar. She sup-

posed that he would stand out anywhere as he was so
tall—a rangy six feet or more—but, whoever he was,
he had a presence that was nothing to do with his
height. Somehow he appeared more sharply in focus
than anyone else around him—at least to her subjective
vision—as if the character so evident in the quirkily
attractive dark face invested him with that sharp, clear
outline.

Obeying some inner instinct that insisted on seeing
the untinted reality, Lucia removed her sunglasses, but
learned nothing further. He was dark, he was probably
in his early thirties, and he was dead sexy.

With his attention being wholly given to a glamorous
young woman with dark red hair, she was unable to
discover the colour of his eyes from where she stood,
here on the fringes of the throng, but she could see
arrogance in the aquiline curve of his nose, while his
mouth was many things—firm, controlled, sensual, and
yet a little harsh, until he smiled at something the girl
with him was saying and the harshness vanished.

With her own eyes no longer hidden by dark lenses,
Lucia became aware of a rippling murmur of recognition in both English and French from several people
close by.

'The Flanders girl.'

'Lucia. . .'

It amused her to know that it was her eyes by which
she was recognised when she didn't think much of them
herself because they were neither blue nor green but
something between the two. She would have preferred
one or the other to such an indeterminate mixture.

An ensuing silence, so absolute as to be breathless
startled her momentarily, but then she was distracted
again, because the man who had caught her attention
was now staring straight at her, as if alerted by the
murmurs that had preceded this strangely avid hush.

She couldn't think of a word that described his

eyes—unless she settled for 'smoke'. Their colour was as much an enigma as their expression, shadowed and secret, and yet something there made her instantly conscious of herself as a woman, automatically picturing the way she must look to him. Of course, the simple, sleeveless white dress, with its round neckline and softly gathered skirt, would flatter her more in a week or two, when she had got her light, honey-coloured tan back and her straight, fine, shoulder-length hair was fair again, instead of the light brown to which her recent lengthy stint of studying indoors had dulled it.

Lucia gave the man the tiniest of contained smiles and caused her gaze to move on casually. She had looked quite long enough for an engaged, soon-to-be-married woman.

A moment later she was forced to return her attention to him, warned by the stir of interest that she detected among those people nearest to her.

He was coming over to her, his long legs giving him a lithe, easy stride, and his face was lit with a smile that gave every indication of delight.

'Lucia!' the voice matched the smile. 'You made it after all.'

Astonishment barely allowed her to register that the smoky eyes were sparkling with enjoyment as he reached her. Then amazement gave way to pure shock as he took her by the shoulders, turning her slightly so that her startled expression was concealed from the group of onlookers. She was five feet seven so he had to bend his head to brush a kiss across her cheek.

Lucia was aware of warmth both from his lips and the body so close to hers, its nearness an invasion when he was a total stranger, however welcoming.

'What. . .' she began faintly, her voice trailing away as she became conscious of something else—an urgency about the way his fingers were biting into her shoulders, their grasp somehow imperative.

'Please excuse us a minute.' He threw the perfunctory request at a small cluster of spectators, and then he was moving her out through one of the Moorish-style archways bordering the large courtyard with its tubs and hanging baskets of lush foliage and the covered bar at one end.

Caught off balance, Lucia couldn't resist until they had rounded a corner and were alone, when she wrenched herself free of his hold and turned to face him indignantly, her heart's rhythm still a speedy drumbeat of surprise.

'What do you think you're doing, accosting me like this? Abducting me?' she demanded furiously.

'Do you always exaggerate?' he enquired amusedly.

'No, only when absolute strangers give me an exaggeratedly warm welcome,' she retorted.

'The situation called for drastic measures,' he asserted rather coolly.

'Oh, I agree! Slapping your face wouldn't be too drastic under the circumstances! Who are you, anyway?' she asked tempestuously, noting that his smile had gone.

'Rob Ballard,' he supplied. 'And it's just as well you didn't come out with that question back there at the party.'

The magnate himself, she realised, trying to remember what she knew about him. But the only thing she could recall was his Zimbabwean nationality and the fact that his hotels had a reputation for luxury and casual elegance.

'And you, of course, are Lucia Flanders,' he added, with a swift, raking assessment of her heart-shaped face, its delicate bone-structure creating gentle curves that cast soft shadows here and there.

'Well, look, Mr Ballard—'

'I think you're going to have to call me Rob, you know,' he cut in with soft significance, accompanying it with another smile, brilliantly slashing this time.

'I'd forgotten about men,' Lucia murmured obscurely. His tone had given her a clue as to what this was about, and she spent a moment reflecting that during the last couple of months she had forgotten about most of the things that pleased, amused or even infuriated her. 'Sorry, *Rob*—but look! Engaged!'

With a piquant smile she held up her hand, displaying the flashing diamond on a plain gold band, and the smoke-coloured eyes narrowed briefly.

'Are you sure of that?' The smile had grown slightly cruel. 'Take it off, Lucia.'

He was reaching for her hand so she dropped it hastily, a little disconcerted by his manner but still confident that she could handle this, even if he was using lines that were unfamiliar to her. She shook her head slowly.

'I've worn it too long,' she claimed happily.

'Way too long when you haven't placed a wedding band beside it,' he agreed smoothly.

'That's due to happen shortly,' she informed him easily, deciding abruptly that she didn't need to make the rejection kind when he was so over-confident. 'So you're out of luck, aren't you?'

'What? Do you think I'm making some kind of pass?' he asked disbelievingly.

It rocked her, because that was exactly what she had thought, but pride came to her rescue and she managed to mask her embarrassment.

'What was it, then?' she demanded. 'That warm welcome when we've never met before—what were you doing?'

'Securing my sister's happiness, or at least her peace of mind—and coincidentally saving your face, I suspect,' Rob Ballard submitted expressionlessly, and paused. 'Didn't Beth Olivier at least give you some warning when she last visited South Africa?'

'What are you talking about?'

Suddenly Lucia's voice was sharp with anxiety. Thierry's mother was a South African who visited her country several times a year, but she had never once contacted Lucia when she'd done so.

Lucia had always been aware of her future mother-in-law's disapproval, and when all her most winning efforts had failed to achieve any softening in her she had accepted the situation, respectful of the breeding which caused Beth to ignore her when she could and be coldly polite when she couldn't, because an open, ongoing quarrel would have been intolerable.

'You've stayed away too long, Lucia. Thierry Olivier obviously got tired of waiting for you, because he and my young sister are on the point of announcing their engagement. That's what this afternoon's party is about, and partly why I'm here.'

He made no attempt to soften it—the brutal announcement was thrown at her with a trace of mockery but nothing else whatsoever.

'I don't believe you.' The denial was automatic. 'Thierry and I have been in love for years, and engaged all this last year.'

'Too long, as I've said.' He was taunting.

'He knew there was no point in our getting married when I couldn't be here living with him. I had to get my degree,' Lucia explained, her tone growing almost blithe as confidence reasserted itself.

'Of course, and you've just completed your third and final year at the University of Witwatersrand, I'm told. So perhaps he decided someone who would put his needs before her career suited him better,' came the derisive suggestion.

'I'd like to hear that from him,' she retorted, beginning to move forward.

'Where do you think you're going?'

'To find Thierry and ask him what's going on,' she snapped, but stopped and took a step backwards as she saw Rob Ballard's hands raised to halt her departure, finding that she didn't want him to touch her.

'Oh, no, Lucia, you are not going to go through there and cause a scene,' he advised her with silken authority. 'But, in a minute or two, you are going to join the party with me and ease my sister's mind by showing her and everyone else that you don't care, that, if anything, this is the way out you've been looking for—ever since you met me, I think we'll make it.'

'And where would I have met you?' Lucia enquired scornfully, but a gathering uneasiness was nudging at her confidence and a tiny crease had appeared between eyebrows which were a shade or two darker than her hair.

'I spent a week in Johannesburg on business a couple of months ago, which is where you've been at university. And, for all anyone knows, I'm in and out of there quite regularly. I've hardly even had a chance to talk to my sister since I arrived here, so she won't wonder why I haven't mentioned you.'

Lucia stared at him with eyes that were beginning to blaze.

'The thing is full of flaws—'

'We'll make it up as we go along.'

'We won't make anything up! You're forgetting something.' Abruptly her fury erupted. 'Even if one word of what you say is true, I happen to be wearing the engagement ring Thierry gave me, and he has not asked me to remove it, or to release him in any way whatsoever.'

'Yes, I had a suspicion that that was the way things were when one of the local people employed here blurted out that he felt so sorry for you. And Olivier was vague about his previous engagmenet when I questioned him about it. Unfortunately I did it in my sister's presence as I couldn't really credit that he'd be so stupid as to be engaged to two women at once. I could see her growing uneasy.

'He didn't even mention your name—I got that from Hassan Mohammed—so she won't wonder at my failure to mention the coincidence when she realises who you are, and I know she'll have questioned Olivier about you by now.'

'Sorry for me!' Lucia's face had flamed at the phrase and she had barely absorbed the rest of his words. 'No one has any need to feel sorry for me! If any of this is true, then this girl, your sister—what's her name?'

'Nadine.'

'She has stolen Thierry from me and I'm going to get him back! Let me past, please!'

Past him was the only way she could go, she had discovered, because a semicircle of close-growing frangipanis blocked her way in all other directions.

'You'd want him back when he has treated you like this?' He was deeply contemptuous. 'Everything else is understandable, but his failure to end one engagement before contracting another is mind-boggling. Presumably he couldn't know how well you'd time your arrival—or how badly, depending on who is looking at it—and was intending to tell you when the new one was an acomplished fact.'

'And you think this man is a suitable husband for your precious sister?' Lucia flared, long acquaintance enabling her to understand Thierry's behaviour—*if* any of this was true.

'It's complicated, and my absence is delaying the announcement,' he returned impatiently. 'It's enough to say that he suits her, and I happen to think that she'll suit him better than you would. It's obvious to me that you've been a weakening influence there as it's only in relation to you that he seems to become less than a man, whereas with regard to my sister I'm satisfied that he is what she needs—strong without being oppressive. Take off that ring, Lucia.'

His eyes had fallen to her hands in which she still held her sunglasses, her fingers twisting and turning tensely. Following his gaze, Lucia forced them to be still.

'And because that's your opinion I must simply give him up?' she taunted. 'If any of this is true.'

'Why would I invent something like this?'

Yes, why? The simple question forced her to accept that he was probably telling the truth, and her face went still and closed as she looked away, staring unseeingly at one of the massive old baobabs that grew here on Grande Comore as they did on the African mainland to the west.

In a short while, when the sun's reunion with the horizon began to streak the sky with lemon and amber, the giant bats of the Comoros, which hung motionless in such trees by day, would begin to emerge, but for now the sun was still a dazzling disc in the blue sky, as bright as the diamond on her finger, and the breeze that caressed her skin was tropically warm; the chill that she was beginning to feel was strictly an interior one and clashed oddly with the heat of rage.

If Thierry truly had done this to her. . .! The combination of pride and sensitivity that was such an intrinsic part of her nature made the humiliation unendurable, and she thought that she hated this man—this Rob Ballard—for having been the one to deal her the humiliation, knowing, as he had to, that she hadn't seen it coming; and knowing too that a man had so little regard for her that he had left her to learn of his rejection from a stranger, which was how it would appear to Rob.

Assaulted by a sudden, panicky suspicion that she must be revealing all the anger and shame just beginning to manifest themselves, Lucia hastily put her sunglasses on before looking at him again.

Such a short while ago, before all this, Rob's dark individuality had been appealing, even arresting—loving Thierry hadn't diminished her healthy appreciation of personality and sex appeal—but she could no longer find anything attractive about him.

Viewing him now, from behind concealing dark lenses, all she could see was the enemy, tall and dark, the fit lines of his body relaxed beneath the casual but obviously good-quality shirt and trousers that he wore. And yet at the same time he gave the impression of being on the alert and in control, ready to deal with anything.

She hoped that she would never have to see him again. Lucia started to remove her ring, her shaking fingers a betrayal now that rage was a buffeting storm within her.

'Don't touch me!' she ordered him furiously when she found her hand in his as he took over the operation.

'I know!' He was sardonically comprehending. 'Right now you're very busy hating me, aren't you? I'm the messenger, and you want to kill me. Illogical but inevitable!'

His perspicacity infuriated her still further. 'You enjoyed being the messenger!'

'Someone had to be.' He didn't deny the accusation, but his expression had hardened. 'I'll keep this for you.'

He had slid the ring from her finger quite easily, and Lucia couldn't honestly feel its removal as a loss since she wasn't really accustomed to its light embrace, having preferred not to wear it on campus, especially as her course had entailed so much laboratory work.

'Give it to me,' she demanded, seeing him slip it into the breast-pocket of his dark green shirt.

'I will when you've calmed down sufficiently not to

make it a prop in a public performance.' He ignored
the hand that she stretched out to him while her other
one was busily opening the small bag that hung on a
strap from her shoulder. 'Then you can give it back to
Olivier some time when my sister isn't around, or
throw it back at him if that's what you prefer. Unless
you'd like me to do it for you?'

'He's not getting it back,' Lucia stated tautly. 'He
gave it to me. It's mine and I'll do as I please with it.'

'Ah! You're going to be theatrical and hurl it into
the sea,' he guessed, a gleam of amusement appearing
in his mysteriously coloured eyes.

'I'm going to flog it and keep the money,' she correct
him impulsively. The reasoning behind her defiance
was somewhat confused, except that if Thierry really
had done this to her he didn't merit any grand gestures.

Rob's amusement had increased. 'Very practical.
Now, try to look as if we've just enjoyed a passionate
reunion and we'll join the party.'

Lucia hesitated, making a business of closing her bag
to give herself time to think, although she already knew
that she had no option. Intense pride was reminding
her that several people who knew her had seen her
arrival. If she failed to reappear they would guess why
with some accuracy, and she could no more bear the
idea of being the subject of pitying gossip than she
could have endured public ridicule.

Lifting her head, she looked at Rob Ballard and said
tightly, 'The act is unnecessary—I couldn't enjoy a
passionate anything with you—but all right, let's go.'

'Then smile,' he adjured indifferently, and stood
aside to allow her to precede him.

The only passion he aroused in her was passionate
dislike, she reflected, with rather desperate humour. It
occurred to her that she ought to be grateful to him for
saving her from making a fool of herself by intercepting
her search for Thierry. Lucia's face burned as she

entertained a picture of herself finding Thierry, innocently inviting his embrace and being publicly rejected,
but the fact that she had something for which to thank
Rob Ballard only exacerbated her resentment.

As they joined the crowd in the beautiful, big courtyard she felt his arm slide about her waist, and she
stiffened.

'I said there was no need for that,' she reminded him
stiltedly. 'Let go.'

'When I'm sure I can trust you to behave.'

'Won't your wife or girlfriend object?' she asked
tartly, chagrined to find herself curious about his personal situation. Her reaction was partly in response to
the looks that he was drawing from just about every
woman around—those who caught his attention offering smiles of unmistakable invitation and a favoured
few winning themselves answering smiles that were
undeniably charming.

'I don't have a wife, and my girlfriends are all very
understanding,' he murmured smoothly.

'I suppose they have to be,' she countered, thinking
that his answer told her a lot, 'or they rapidly become
ex-girlfriends.'

'I travel a lot,' he offered dismissively, as if in
explanation.

Lucia was having difficulty with her breathing. She
knew that it was because she was on edge, dreading the
moment when she saw Thierry and would know if he
had really done this thing to her, but it was easier to
blame Rob for the tight, breathless sensation afflicting
her.

'Don't hold me so tight,' she muttered angrily.

'Don't worry, Lucia, it's not personal,' he responded
in a low voice for her ears only. 'I'm not especially
attracted to girls like you.'

'And I don't like men like you,' she retaliated
promptly.

'Great.' He gave her a sharply scintillating smile. 'We should get on perfectly.'

'Or not at all—'

She broke off as her eyes encountered a bright red-gold head some distance away, and a tiny sound of acute distress escaped her as she looked for and found the young woman clinging to Thierry Olivier's arm. The nightmare was real.

The arm about her waist tightened, reminding her of the urgency with which Rob's fingers had grasped her shoulders when he had first accosted her.

'You'll be all right,' he asserted in a hard voice.

'I know I will,' she flared.

'And your heart isn't breaking.' Rob was openly taunting now, as if he actually wanted her furious.

'No!'

Inwardly she was coming apart, but she would never admit it, never show it to anyone, and least of all to this man who had already seen too much of her; who had seen her openly disbelieving when he had told her the truth, and who must now feel only pity or contempt—either of which were anathema to all that was proud and sensitive in her.

'Because you didn't really love him.' His smile was savagely derisive this time.

'Because I know I can get him back,' she contradicted, in an absolute rage with him and the world, and saying just anything. 'If I want him. I'm not sure that I do.'

Rob's eyes had narrowed, and it was a moment before he spoke, observing idly, 'You definitely don't need him.'

'I don't *need* anyone!'

It was pride driving her to make these wild claims, because it was all she had now, and no one must guess at the humiliation that was scalding her.

'That's one thing I knew about you before I'd even

set eyes on you,' Rob commented in a tone of agreement.

Lucia ignored that, forcing her lips into the shape of a smile as she became aware that several people nearby were regarding them curiously, although Thierry was not yet aware of her presence.

'So that's her—your sister?' she prompted in a low, taut voice, staring at the woman whose colouring was the only thing she appeared to have in common with her brother, and whose oval face was still and serene.

'Nadine,' he confirmed, 'who does need Olivier. So you're going to let her have him, aren't you? Your hands, Lucia.'

Only then did she become aware that her hands were clasped in front of her, their tense fingers twisting and turning agitatedly again, and she flushed, forcing them free of each other and letting them drop to her sides.

She didn't care; she wouldn't care, she told herself frantically. She wouldn't let these people destroy her— Thierry and that woman, and this man who saw too much and knew how devastated she really was.

'How did they meet?' she asked, managing a netural tone despite the unevenness of her breathing.

'Nadine has been working here at the hotel.'

'Nepotism,' Lucia accused smartly, intent on keeping him the main focus of her anger because somehow it seemed safer that way under the present circumstances.

'She knows the business. She did a course at the hotel school in Johannesburg.' Rob made it sound as if he was being incredibly magnanimous, bothering to enlighten her that much, but then he gave her a hawkishly challenging look.

'Strange! Hassan Mohammed didn't mention gratuitously opinionated and critical. "Such a vivacious, sunny-natured, loving girl" were his exact words, but perhaps something is traditionally blinding him.'

Lucia knew Hassan well. He had clearly been exaggerating, but she supposed that the description could apply loosely. When she wasn't wounded in pride and heart, she liked and got on with people.

She had felt a pang of envy when Rob had mentioned his sister's training. Because it involved dealing with people, the hotel industry had always attracted her, and she had been looking for some unhurtful way to tell her father that she wanted to go to the hotel school rather than getting her degree when the unexpected, fatal heart attack had hit, and there had only been time for a loving urge to ease his final minutes with a promise to go for the degree that meant so much to him.

She had done it, confident that when the results came out she would have passed. And she had come back to the Comoros to fulfil her promise to Thierry, knowing that she was unlikely ever to have to use her qualifications for a number of reasons—including Thierry's reactionary dislike of the idea of a wife who worked, unless it was to help him on the estate.

Nevertheless, she had come intent on requesting a few weeks in which to unwind after the mental pressures of the last year before they started planning their wedding, and she'd been hopeful that he would be agreeable to her at least taking a temporary job at one or other of the new hotels' which had been erected on the island in proof of international faith in the Comoros' burgeoning popularity as a holdiay destination.

However briefly, she yearned to experience more of the sort of contact for which she had acquired a taste in South Africa, earning her air fares between Johannesburg and Grande Comore by waitressing at a restaurant in the evenings and working on the tills of an up-market chain store on Saturdays and Sunday mornings.

Now it occurred to her that, without Thierry, a job was a dire necessity as she hadn't bothered to save a full return fare this year. In effect, she was stranded here, and not even a national. She could only have become Comorean when they'd married, gaining a proper national identity at last, plus the sense of belonging that she imagined must come with being settled and part of a pair.

Lucia sent Rob Ballard an oblique look from behind her sunglasses.

'She won't be working once she marries Thierry,' she ventured.

'She has quit already.' His glance was slightly curious.

'Then—' She hesitated, but the urge to phrase it antagonistically wouldn't be suppressed. 'She has got my man, so can I have her job? Or any job?'

'You'll have to apply to Personnel, or ask Chester Watson—the manager here,' he elaborated, seeing her blank look. 'They do the hiring and firing and I don't interfere. I'll introduce you to Chester in a minute as I'll have to leave you to announce this engagement for the happy couple, and I don't want you anywhere near them until you've got yourself under better control than you have now.

'But why don't you go back to South Africa and get a job? The Comoros aren't really your home.'

'They were going to be. Neither is South Africa, and I barely remember England because we moved around the Indian Ocean most of my life. My mother tried to persuade me to go back with her and study in England after my father died, but Johannesburg was nearer and cheaper, and by that time Thierry and I had fallen in. . .' Her words faded as Lucia realised that what she was describing was an illusion. 'My father was—'

'Ernest Flanders, the marine biologist,' Rob supplied, when she broke off again as she wondered why she was bothering to confide anything at all. 'He made some impressive discoveries, and it seems that you're set to continue his work eventually as it's marine biology you've been studying, isn't it? Johannesburg always strikes me as an incongruous place to do it, inland as it is, but, of course, Wits degrees are recognised worldwide.

'Hotel work seems a bit of a waste for you. Why don't you go back and find something that will utilise your specialised knowledge?'

She was surprised that he should know so much about her, but she didn't dwell on it, riled by an awareness that his advice was far from being disinterested—proffered for his sister's sake rather than hers. He wanted her off the island.

'Why? Are you afraid I'll embarrass Thierry and your sister if I hang around?' she challenged defiantly. 'That I'll cause trouble—try to get Thierry back?'

'And succeed? Haven't you learnt anything this afternoon about the dangers of being over-confident?' Rob derided with deliberate cruelty, and Lucia was very glad of her darkened lenses, because while she could keep her mouth in the shape of a smile she had no control over anything her eyes might be revealing.

'Go back to South Africa or home to England, Lucia. There's no suitable work for you here, and at this stage of your career, fresh out of university, no research organisation or publisher is going to give you the sort of funding your father must have had to be free to roam around the ocean for so many years.'

'I'm staying,' Lucia insisted, wishing that she could come up with some dignified reason for doing so, hating the idea of his knowing just *how* stupidly over-confident she had been in coming back to the island without giving any consideration to the possibility that Thierry might no longer want her and that she would be left trapped here, unable to afford to leave.

'If I can't get a job here, I'll try somewhere else— one of the other hotels, probably.'

He studied her in silence for several seconds, his eyes

very hard. Then he shrugged. 'Do as you please, but I think you should bear in mind that if you make any attempt to sabotage my sister's relationship with Thierry Olivier I will make you regret it.'

The arm round her waist took on the quality of steel, so she was perplexed by his sudden, flirtatiously caressing smile until he added authoritatively, 'Don't stop smiling, Lucia. Olivier has just seen you, and he and Nadine are both looking this way now.'

'I don't want to speak to them yet.'

She couldn't keep a panicky note out of her voice. Even if no one else guessed what she was going through, Thierry should, and the thought was unbearable. She couldn't even bring herself to look in his direction for the moment.

'Until you've planned your strategy?' Rob mocked. 'You won't have to speak to them. I'll take you over to meet Chester Watson now, and then I'll go and make the great announcement for them, as that's the way my sister wants it. But just remember what I've said. No trouble—no spoiling her day, please, Lucia.'

CHAPTER TWO

LUCIA's face ached from smiling and smiling as she pretended that she didn't care, but the glass of champagne that Rob had taken from a tray borne by a passing waiter and handed to her had a tendency to shake if she didn't concentrate.

It was difficult to concentrate on anything at all when her inner turmoil was so distracting, but she was determined not to let anyone know how shaken she was so she kept on smiling, forcing herself to talk sociably when she was introduced to Chester Watson— an attractive, stocky Englishman whom Rob said the Ballard Group had poached from one of Kenya's most famous hotels.

It was obvious that Chester held his employer in high esteem, and Lucia saw why. Their conversation touching briefly on hotel business at one point, Rob became very much the high-powered tycoon, decisive and commanding, but without being condescending, looking at Chester as he spoke, using his name and soliciting his opinion.

They were soon joined by the young woman in whose company she had first seen Rob. Madelon Brouard was a few years older than Lucia, glamorous and sufficiently sophisticated to be able to reveal her interest in Rob without being crass about it in any way, even when he had his arm round another woman's waist.

'Incidentally, Chester, Lucia thinks she'd like a job here,' Rob mentioned after the introductions were completed.

'You would love it, Lucia,' Madelon immediately put in enthusiastically. 'I work in the hotel shop. It is the best employment I have had, and I have done most sorts of work. I was infected so badly by the wanderlust that I could not go home to take up my place at university when the one year of travelling I promised to myself ended. So here I stand, unqualified for all but casual labour to this day. But I have learned several languages and had many wonderful experiences. Did I say, Rob? Chester talks of moving me into Nadine's post.'

'So you won't be replacing Nadine, Lucia,' Rob said significantly, with a mocking smile that added silently, Although Nadine has replaced you in another area.

'In fact, I've an idea that we might have something unique for you, Lucia,' Chester told her. 'In view of who you are—Ernest Flanders' daughter—and your own special interest and abilities. Oh, yes, I've heard a lot about you since I've been here. You have fans on the island, it seems, and, of course, your father is remembered with admiration.'

'I'm sure I can be useful,' Lucia submitted eagerly. 'And, while I can't match Madelon's several languages, I am as fluent in French as in English, because when we weren't living in the Comoros we'd often be in places like Mauritius, Réunion and the Seychelles, and I usually had to attend French schools.'

'And you get on with people?' Chester probed.

'Very well,' she claimed confidently, and was piqued by Rob's sceptical smile.

Well, of course he was an exception. What else did he expect when he had been the bearer of bad news, delivering it with more sadistic enjoyment than compassion? Not that she wanted his sympathy, or anyone else's either—

It was at this point in her angry thoughts that Rob removed his arm from around her waist, and Lucia was subject to a moment's sheer, unreasoning panic in response to the loss of its warmth and, she realised belatedly, its support.

'Will you excuse me, please? Nadine is sending out agitated signals so I'd better go and play my part. I won't be long, angel,' he added to Lucia, his tone indulgent. 'Chester and Madelon will look after you.'

Furious, she would have told him that she didn't need looking after if it hadn't been for the inhibiting presence of the other two.

So it was shaming that his departure should leave her feeling so oddly bereft, but she would have died rather than show it. She watched him go, attracting as he always did much feminine attention and rewarding it with the occasional smile when eye contact was made, but she thought that she knew where his real interest lay, as it was with Madelon that she had first seen him.

Lucia turned to Chester Watson determinedly. The manager just had time to relieve her mind by assuring her that employment at the hotel included board and lodging if required, when someone interrupted, demanding his urgent attention.

'Perhaps you'll come and see me tomorrow morning and I'll tell you what I've got in mind, Lucia?' he suggested quickly. 'I really must deal with this now, unfortunately.'

'I like him, but it is Rob Ballard I find attractive.' With both men gone, Madelon seized the opportunity to indulge in girl-talk. 'You too? I heard something, that you were engaged to Thierry Olivier previously, but Rob is much more exciting. I am not criticising your former choice, you understand, and Thierry is beautiful, but Rob is more—more of a man! You have known him long?'

'A while,' Lucia responded ambiguously, liking Madelon and aware that at any other time she would probably have been quite happy to play the rating game, however pointless it really was when taste was such a subjective thing.

She hadn't meant to make use of the fiction that Rob had established, her pride rebelling at the idea of needing anyone's help or co-operation to get her through this ordeal, but she shrank from admitting that until a short while ago she had believed that she still was engaged to Thierry.

'Not long enough to let him go?' Madelon prompted mock-hopefully. 'But perhaps he will come here more frequently and remain longer if you are here, and everything is fair, do you admit? We will have fun!'

Several people who remembered Lucia began to drift up and greet her, and once again she found herself tacitly participating in the charade that Rob had initiated, smiling determinedly as they made knowing comments about her having landed a bigger fish, apparently under the impression that they were using a wittily appropriate pun.

Lucia felt ashamed of herself, but knowing the truth would have made them as uncomfortable as she would have been in telling, if the relief and happiness they all evinced at seeing her apparently unperturbed by the occasion were anything to go by.

The fact that they had obviously been concerned for her produced further emotional conflict for Lucia. She was touched to know they cared, but that they had needed to care was humiliating.

Finally, when a hush had fallen and Rob was making a simple announcement of the engagement of his sister Nadine to Thierry Olivier, Lucia made herself look once more at the man who had let her in for all this.

It was a shock to find Thierry looking at *her*, but she kept right on smiling, and after a moment she saw his gaze drop, apparently to her hands, now tensely locked round the stem of her glass, and then an incomprehensible mixture of expressions flitted over his sensitive features, presumably in reaction to the absence of her ring.

Thierry! Lucia was rigid with rage and hurt, but she understood why he had done it this way. Thierry was a sensitive yet passive man, abhorring emotional conflict in particular and too much raw emotion generally.

Even in the first flush of their youthful love just over three years ago, he had been uncomfortable with her grief over her father's sudden death, staying away from her until he could be sure that she had it under control. Now it occurred to her that these traits had become more pronounced over the years; he had come to rely on her for so much, touchingly confident in her ability to deal with any unpleasantness on his behalf.

Lucia remembered the day that seemed to symbolise that reliance, when his beloved dog had run in front of one of the island water-carrier vehicles, and he had been utterly unable even to look at the poor animal, begging her to take it away, to find help for it if it was still alive, throwing down his car-keys for her and retreating.

She supposed that some people would have called that weak, but she had seen it as a measure of his faith in her. She understood and loved him—and now she had lost him. There wasn't going to be any wedding, or a home that wasn't borrowed or rented, or the security of knowing that she could stay put and never have to think about moving on.

She was doing it again, Lucia realised—the thing that had begun to disturb her over the last year, thinking of marriage to Thierry in terms of having a home. Well, neither marriage nor a home was any longer on the agenda, so she wasn't going to worry about it now.

Abruptly, accepting the reality, Lucia raised her glass along with everyone else and toasted the newly engaged couple, her gaze resting a moment on the girl

whom Thierry had preferred to her and then straying
to the man whom Madelon had called 'more of a man'.

True enough, if you believed that manliness
embraced insensitivity and an unwarranted sense of
superiority. Right now Rob Ballard was probably con-
gratulating himself on having saved the day for his
sister.

'You must be thirsty!' Madelon laughed from beside
her, and, looking down, Lucia realised that she had
unthinkingly drained her glass. The champagne was
available because hotels which catered for foreign
visitors were exempt from the Koran-based laws of the
archipelago. 'I too. I will find a waiter.'

Madelon took her empty glass away and Lucia went
on staring at Rob, hating him for being the only person
to know how this had hit her.

'Lucia.'

The coolly polite greeting had her turning to confront
Thierry's widowed mother, as trimly immaculate as
ever.

Although a light, in-flight meal was the only thing
that she had eaten all day, the champagne couldn't
have gone to her head this quickly, but Lucia felt her
smile widening outrageously, and the words that
emerged from her mouth carried more expression than
she had ever before permitted herself in addressing this
woman.

'Beth! Congratulations! This must be an amazingly
happy day for you.'

'Oh, it is,' Beth Olivier agreed smoothly. 'Especially
as I see you're taking it so well. But then, judging by
the company I saw you in earlier, you've found someone to distract you—and probably not for the first time
over the years. So, all in all, Rob Ballard has been a
force for good, although I still have to deplore these
big, new hotels, spoiling the coastline and doing who
knows what damage to the environment.'

'The environmental impact studies were favourable to their erection,' Lucia pointed out, finding a perverse relish in the realisation that she no longer had to be so careful not to disagree with Beth—at least Thierry had done her one favour!

'And unless you want to return to the barter system, or cowries for currency, their presence benefits the local people and the economy in all sorts of ways, not least by providing employment, doesn't it? I still remember the high incidence of *kwashiorkor* among the island children the first time my parents and I lived here, in the mid-eighties. Hopefully that's becoming history.'

'Darling.' Rob had joined them in time to hear her words, putting a casual arm across Lucia's shoulders and addressing Beth as he continued, 'I'm discovering that Lucia is incredibly loyal—always ready to defend me.'

His tone and smile were so indulgent that Lucia was disconcerted, needing to remind herself that it was all an act.

'Oh, I suppose I have to forgive you, Rob, since it has been the Ballard Group's venture here that enabled my son to meet someone so ideally suited to him,' Beth allowed rather coyly, preparing to move on.

'Well, I don't suppose I'll be seeing much of you, Lucia. I think it would be better if you didn't come round to the estate at all, don't you? Misguided though it was, we can't get away from the fact that Thierry and you were once an item, and we don't want to distress dear Nadine, do we? She's staying with us, of course. I'm sure Rob agrees with me.'

'Lucia is going to be too busy to have much time for casual socialising anyway,' Rob claimed, with so much caressing significance that Lucia stiffened resentfully, effectively distracted from the additional humiliation of hearing that she was unwelcome in the Olivier home.

Still further distraction was provided by the way his fingers were now stirring idly against the smooth skin of her upper arm, their warmth and the light movement producing an inner frisson of awareness, so she hardly noticed Beth's departure.

'Stop it,' she finally managed in a sharp little voice, moving out of his reach.

'I told you, it's not personal, Lucia,' he drawled, the taunting challenge sparkling in the smoky eyes making them as brilliant as gems, and as hard. 'But there is one thing about you that has actually succeeded in arousing my interest, and that's your defence of the sort of controversial progress that goes with the tourist industry. Biologists aren't usually part of the backlash against green concerns.'

'And I'm not! I just happen to think people are the most important living things on the planet,' she snapped. 'Will you excuse me, please, and apologise to Madelon for me? She was getting more champagne, but I see someone has detained her.'

'Where are you going?' Rob demanded, as arrogantly as if he had the right to know.

'To fetch my luggage from the Olivier estate, as that's where I left it and since Beth Olivier has just made it crystal-clear that I am no longer welcome there.'

Lucia was horrified to hear her voice trembling with the rage that she felt against the things that had been done to her today. It should have been one of the happiest days of her life—her returning at last without the prospect of yet another departure and another year's exile lurking a month or two ahead.

'I'll get a car and drive you there,' Rob said.

'Don't bother,' she returned rebelliously. 'Presumably Thierry and *dear* Nadine will be here a while yet, so I can be in and out while this party is still going on.'

'I'll drive you,' he repeated calmly.

'Why?' she asked defiantly. 'If "dear" Nadine doesn't know anything about it, she's not in danger of being upset, and that's why you interfered in the first place, isn't it? You weren't rescuing *me*.'

'Not intentionally, but as you appear to have taken advantage of the impression I set out to create, at least to the extent of refraining from saying or doing anything to contradict it, it seems that I *was* in fact rescuing you,' he observed mockingly. 'But let's leave and get your luggage before your current mood leads you to shatter the illusion and waste all the effort you've put in.'

'Thereby upsetting "dear" Nadine,' Lucia added tartly, her hostility leaping in response to the insight which enabled him to recognise the present fragility of her control.

'Listen to yourself, Lucia,' Rob advised her on an iron note of warning. 'Come on, let's go— What is it?'

She had made a small sound of exasperated realisation, and now she hesitated, trying to work out if the little money she still had available to her would stretch to the sort of prices that she guessed most of the new hotels would charge.

'Chester Watson was called away before he could tell me what he has in mind for me, so I'm not actually employed here yet, when bed and board will be available to me. I'll need to book a room for tonight if there's a vacancy,' she admitted, trying to sound casual about it.

'We'll organise something if there isn't. But it can wait until we get back from the Olivier place.'

'This thing really is full of holes,' Lucia accused resentfully a few minutes later, when she was seated beside him in the sort of up-market French car which would have been a rarity on the island not so many years ago. 'The housekeeper could give everything away.'

Rob slanted her a calculating look. 'D'you think she can be persuaded or bribed not to?'

Lucia shrugged. 'It's possible, if she thinks she's doing Beth down in some way. Beth has never been exactly popular with any of her housekeepers. That's why they change so often.'

At least she didn't have to worry about sounding disloyal now that Beth was no longer destined to be her mother-in-law, she reflected drily.

'I understand she's planning to go and live in South Africa once she's seen her son safely married to Nadine,' Rob commented.

Her brief laugh had a brittle sound. 'She wouldn't even consider it when I was the one he was marrying.'

'Because she saw the damage you were doing him, and she's a devoted mother,' he suggestesd brutally. 'It's obvious that she dislikes you, but Nadine really will suit him better than you.'

'Nadine can hardly know him yet,' she claimed furiously. 'And how well does she understand him? He's a passive man for a start—the kind who turns the other cheek, if you know what I mean.'

'Yes, and that passivity was becoming a weakness when he had a character like you willing to run his life for him. I sensed both resentment and shame in his attitude while he was busy hedging about his relationship with you. With Nadine he'll be able to feel like a man again. You were obviously emasculating him,' Rob asserted contemptuously.

'What do you know about any of it?' Lucia demanded tempestuously. 'You can barely know Thierry either, and you've only just met me.'

'I know you haven't put him first. You left him for most of three years, didn't you?' he prompted derisively.

'I had to get my degree—' she began.

'Of course you did,' he agreed sardonically. 'Naturally that came first. You're a career woman.'

'I don't believe this! Do you really have some kind of reactionary prejudice against women with careers?' Lucia taunted, genuinely startled.

'No prejudice at all, Lucia,' he corrected her smoothly. 'How can I when so many key positions within the Ballard Group are occupied by your sex? But Thierry Olivier doesn't need a career-orientated woman for his personal partner anymore than I do.'

'You? You're the complete opposite of Thierry.' Sheer astonishment provoked the spontaneous protest, but then she caught herself up. 'For one thing, you're utterly insensitive.'

'And he's so sensitive, leaving you to learn that you've been replaced from whoever might tell you? But add possessiveness to whatever other faults you've decided I have and you'll know why I'd hate to be personally involved with someone who doesn't put me first.'

'I'd call that egotistical,' she argued.

'That too. Whatever, I like warm, generous, emotional women who give all of themselves to a relationship, not just the part that isn't reserved for the pursuit of ambition.'

'I'm really not very interested in knowing what sort of women you like,' Lucia told him dismissively, although just for a moment she had found herself intrigued.

But the exchange had been too personal—an attack on her, in essence—and if he really thought that she was career-obsessed to the exclusion of love then it just showed how little he knew about the whole situation, and she ought to be indifferent to his opinion—as she was!

'And I already know what sort of men you like—

when you can be bothered with them at all,' Rob returned amusedly.

'The same kind dear Nadine likes, obviously—and isn't she going to find it a little difficult to believe you're interested in me?' Lucia added curiously as the question occurred to her. 'She's your sister, so she must know what your tastes are.'

'We'll appear to drift apart in due course.' He was unperturbed. 'Yes, as you've said, the thing has holes in it, but it was the best I could come up with in the necessity of the moment.'

'You're going to find it inconvenient if I insist on maintaining this fiction you've devised,' she ventured maliciously.

'Unfortunately for you, fortunately for me, I won't be around for very long.'

'Then, believe me, I consider myself equally fortunate!'

Said feelingly, it made him laugh, but he didn't take it up. Initially Lucia was relieved to be left to her thoughts, but she swiftly discovered that it had been the challenge he'd presented and the consequent need to keep arguing with him that had kept her strong. Allowed to dwell on what Thierry had done to her, her hold on herself loosened and she weakened rapidly, in danger of breaking down.

Behind the dark lenses, she blinked furiously, and it required an effort to make her lips stop trembling.

'Wait here,' Rob instructed her when they drew up outside the house on the estate that Thierry had inherited from his father. It was a typically French Colonial building, only to be expected as the islands had been French before three of the four had opted for independence in the form of a Federal Islamic Republic, and Thierry's father had been French. 'I'll get your things and talk to the housekeeper. How many pieces of luggage are there?'

She told him jerkily, hating herself for letting him do this without her offering even a token protest; hating herself for having let him take charge in the first place and continue to control the situation, but terrified of all that she might betray if she attempted to speak now.

So she sat there in the car with the window open, a little soothed by the island scents carried on the tropical afternoon breeze, for these were the Perfumed Isles to those who lacked the sense of evolution that made another sobriquet, that of the Coelacanth Isles, equally romantic.

The estate produced ylang-ylang, the base for most perfumes, and from here she could see a small plantation of the trees with their strange, twisted shapes but exotic blooms. Precious woods, vanilla pods, which were an offshoot of the orchid, and the spices for which the islands were famous—cloves, coriander, saffron and more—all played their part in giving Grande Comore its uniquely characteristic fragrance.

From where she was she could also see part of the lower slopes of Mount Karthala, the volcano dominating the island, its past eruptions responsible for the stretches of black rock which alternated with white sands at certain points along the coast and extended beneath the ocean to be visible through the clear turquoise water. The emissions periodically issuing from vents in the mountain's sides were a reminder that it was still active.

Rob Ballard's reappearance distracted her. Lucia watched him striding towards the car, carrying her luggage as effortlessly as if it were weightless. So tall and lithe, he had a loose, easy way of moving that was utterly self-confident, and she felt a surge of hostile emotion that was mostly resentment. It was galling to have to accept help from him, especially under circumstances as embarrassing as these.

She supposed it could be said that she was actually *using* him, since his assistance wasn't really aimed at her at all, but she could take no comfort from the thought. Too much shame was attached to the mere fact that she should *need* to make use of him.

He was smiling sardonically as he got into the car after placing her luggage in the boot.

'You were right; the housekeeper was amenable to forgetting you and your luggage had ever been here. She really entered into the spirit of things, especially after I hinted that you and Madame Olivier are mortal enemies. I gather she's on the verge of seeking employment elsewhere.'

He paused, treating her to brief, raking assessment. 'I also implied that it was me you'd really been looking for, but because we're both Ballard you'd somehow got my whereabouts confused with my sister's.'

'Like a typical dumb blonde,' Lucia supplemented caustically, disgusted with herself for feeling relieved on hearing him.

'You're not exactly blonde,' he observed dismissively as he started the car.

'Give me a few days! I've hardly seen the sun these last few weeks because of my exams.'

'Scarcely the greatest of the sacrifices you've made to your future career,' Rob mocked, the reminder unkind because just for a second or two she had forgotten Thierry, revelling in the awareness that she was at last free of the pressures attendant on keeping her promise to her father.

'As it turns out! How old is this precious sister of yours?' she demanded abruptly.

Catching the antagonistic note, he shot her a contemptuous look.

'Don't blame Nadine. She couldn't have *stolen* Olivier from you unless he wanted to be stolen. He's not that weak. My sister is twenty-five,' he added neutrally.

'Twenty-five?' Lucia repeated with heartfelt outrage. 'And she still needs her big brother going around smoothing the way for her, shielding her from anything that might upset her? I'm only twenty-one and I haven't had anyone looking out for me like that since I was a teenager.'

And she didn't want or need anyone doing so either, did she? Her mother was a remote figure, so, essentially, she had been alone in the world since her father's death—a condition which marriage to Thierry would have ended. Now it looked as if she was going to go on being alone, neither belonging to anyone nor with anyone who belonged to her.

'And look at you now!' he rejoined mercilessly. 'It's none of your business, but Nadine has had some miserable experiences in the past, so she deserves this chance of happiness.

'She has the sort of quiet personality that can invite bullying in certain circumstances, but she won't get that from a non-confrontational character like Olivier, and in return she'll be able to use her particular strength— an instinctive knowledge of the subtle tricks of a very old-fashioned kind of femininity—to boost him. Strange as it seems, the relationship works.'

'Oh, and because of all this—this marriage made in heaven—I really ought to sit back and let her have him?' she challenged indignantly.

'Why not? You don't really want him.' Rob sounded indifferent.

'Perhaps not, but I could still get him back,' she asserted, suddenly in a mood of wild perversity.

Of course she didn't want Thierry back! Not now, when he had proved himself so undeserving of her love, she acknowledged in silent fury; but getting him

back would prove to Rob that she was worth something
as a woman—

Only why should she want to prove it, and to this
man specifically? The only opinion of her that mattered
was her own, and she knew her worth so she had
nothing to prove—nothing at all!

'Try it,' Rob was inviting her softly.

'I just might,' she flung back at him defiantly.

'You'll regret it.'

'Are you threatening me?'

'Yes.' It was silkily ruthless, and she met it with a
brief, scornful laugh. 'Warning you, anyway—and
warning you too that you've got a way to go still before
you're free to give way to tears or a trantrum or
whatever it is you do when you're thwarted, so I suggest
you try to control your pique for the time being.'

Pique! She really and truly hated him, Lucia decided
tempestuously, although not entirely for the way he
was trivialising her feelings, because her pride half-
welcomed that as being preferable to having him know
how badly this had hit her even while her sensitivity
was outraged by his unfeeling attitude.

But how could he know just how precariously she
was teetering on the edge of losing control of her
emotions when he had known her so short a time? It
was infuriating, the way he kept guessing what was
going on in her heart and her head, and guessing so
accurately.

'What's the tariff?' she asked, carefully expressionless, when they reached the hotel, and when he told
her she worked out that she could just afford a night
here, plus, perhaps, a meal this evening, as breakfast
was included. After that she would be broke, so she
just hoped that she would be able to begin whatever
job Chester Watson thought he had for her at once.

'Of course, it would be more appropriate to the
illusion we're trying to establish if I simply installed

you in the suite I use here—and there is a second bedroom,' Rob went on, a gleam of mockery appearing in his eyes as she opened her mouth to protest. 'Relax, Lucia! There's a limit to what I'm prepared to do in my sister's interests. I'm not inflicting you on myself.'

'I wouldn't agree anyway. You can't dislike me half as much as I dislike you,' she flared, automatically removing her sunglasses as they entered the spacious, ultra-modern reception area, and then wishing she hadn't but deciding that it would constitute too much of a betrayal to replace them. 'Oh, hell!'

'What now?' he demanded irritably as she came to a halt.

Lucia had recognised the handsome face and soft dark eyes of one of a trio of young men on duty at the reception counter. She regarded Rob warily.

'Was Hassan Mohammed the employee you said felt sorry for me?' she asked stiffly.

'Yes.' The answer was devoid of sympathy, understanding or even amusement, yet he was looking at her expectantly. 'A past or future interest, Lucia?'

'A *friend*,' she emphasised, wondering what had made him ask such a question, and in that particular tone. He couldn't possibly see her as some sort of *femme fatale*, especially when Thierry had just rejected her!

Lucia drew her shoulders back. So there was to be one last call on her strength today. Her friendship with Hassan went back to the days when they had been childhood playmates, the first time she and her parents had lived on the island. He was one of the kindest people she knew, but she didn't want his pity and he had to be convinced that it was superfluous.

She tilted her chin at an angle, fixed a smile to her face, willing her eyes to be clear and shining, and went forward, aware of Rob Ballard at her side.

Mercifully, Hassan made no reference to Thierry,

being more interested in hearing whether she thought she had passed her exams and telling her how delighted he was to have secured a position here where he was being trained in all aspects of the hotel business.

Once again Lucia was aware of Rob as the dynamic magnate, as it was obvious that Hassan and the other two young men considered themselves honoured by his brief attention when he asked a question or two.

'Lucia may be joining you on the staff temporarily if Chester Watson feels she has something to offer,' Rob told Hassan when the formalities of registering were concluded.

Lucia absorbed the 'temporarily', and she was no longer smiling as they turned and moved away from the counter.

'What are you hanging around for?' she demanded aggressively in a low voice. 'I hope you're not expecting me to thank you?'

'I'd be disappointed if I was, wouldn't I?' he retorted sardonically in an equally low voice. 'Don't worry, you're free of my company as of now. I must get back to the party outside. But, much as we both wish this could be a permanent parting of the ways, I'll need to see you some time tomorrow so we can discuss whether it's necessary for us to continue with this act.'

'It isn't!' she assured him in an intense, hostile whisper, which made his brilliant smile come as a surprise.

But it was only for the benefit of the men at the counter and the handful of other people around, as she realised when he raised his voice and said, 'I'll see you later, angel.'

Then he was striding easily away from her, attracting the usual amount of fascinated attention but ignoring it, presumably intent on taking up with Madelon Brouard where her own inconvenient arrival had forced him to leave off, Lucia decided acidly.

A few minutes later as the young man who had brought her luggage up to her room departed, closing the door quietly behind him, she was alone at long last, the need for pretence over.

The first thought to occur to her came in the form of the belated realisation that Rob still had her engagement ring in his pocket, and she slapped her hand down onto the dressing-table top in a fury of frustration, irrationally inclined to blame him for everything that had gone wrong and all the humiliations that had been inflicted on her this day.

Then, as her shoulders slumped and she collapsed onto a pretty wooden chair, Lucia burst into tears.

CHAPTER THREE

HER shirt dangling from her hand, Lucia stopped to
select a shell from the softly gleaming scatter washed
up by the high tide in the night. Then she continued on
up the dazzling white beach, which she had to herself
at present, stopping when she came to a palm, automatically checking it for the presence of coconuts likely
to fall and then turning to look back at the ocean from
which she had just emerged.

She was an excellent swimmer, but with no one
around to expect an impressive demonstration she had
merely splashed about in the shallow waves close to
shore. Nevertheless, even such modest exercise had left
her hungry and she was looking forward to breakfast.

So, being crossed in love hadn't affected her appe-
tite—unless she was about to turn into a comfort-eater,
she reflected with wry humour.

She had also been ravenous after the storms of angry
weeping the evening before, and had completely finished the meal she had ordered from room service.
Then, exhausted by emotion and with her muscles all
aching as a result of the tension which must have held
her in its grip ever since Rob Ballard had told her
about Thierry's betrayal, she had fallen into a sound,
dreamless sleep, sufficiently healthy to be awake early
in consequence.

The Comorean hot season was just beginning now.
Although a few clouds were racing overhead, the sun
already blazed with a burning heat at this hour of the
morning. Hence her retreat to the shade of the coconut
palms fringing the beach, as she had neglected to apply

any protection to her skin prior to coming out for her early swim.

'Deepest black! Is that in mourning for your lost love?'

The soft, fine sand underfoot had prevented Lucia hearing Rob Ballard's approach, and she spun round in shock as the mocking voice spoke from close by, finding his gaze travelling from the black Indian cotton shirt she held to the plain black one-piece she was wearing cut low at both back and front and high over her hips.

She felt a prick of resentment at his having caught her off guard, acutely conscious that he hadn't been encountering her at her best the previous day either, when shock and fury over Thierry's defection had been affecting her behaviour, causing her to talk wildly, to lash out at him as the bearer of the bad tidings.

'All sympathy, aren't you?' she attacked sarcastically, aware that she would have hated it had he really been sympathetic, preferring his callous derision. 'How did you know I'm not about to jump in the sea and drown myself?'

'Would you bother to dress so alluringly for the occasion? Or I should say undress,' he corrected himself amusedly, his glance skimming the slenderness of her limbs and the subtle curves to which the one-piece clung so faithfully, as he shook his head. 'You're too tough anyway. I can see you in a reckless mood setting out to drown your sorrows. But yourself—no!'

'Is that meant to be a compliment? It just makes me sound thick-skinned, but perhaps you admire people like that, being so insensitive yourself.'

She offered the insult with a wide smile, secretly longing for the concealment of the sunglasses that had served her so well yesterday, but she hadn't bothered to bring them out with her.

The way he was studying her was disconcerting, and she pulled the thin shirt on in an instinctive, defensive reaction, although it was actually only her heart-shaped face, sensitive mouth, and eyes almost the same colour as the sea over which his smoky gaze was roaming now.

The intense black probably did look funereal on her at present, when she was still afflicted by examination pallor—the dull, faded look that came from too much time spent indoors and the diet of coffee and carbohydrates that she had needed to keep going—but the colour suited her when she wasn't so washed out. Right now, with her hair still darkened and flattened by seawater, she probably looked even mousier than she had yesterday.

By contrast Rob looked superbly healthy, vibrantly alive, alert and fit. Lucia ran her eyes over his jeans and white sports shirt, her mind visualising what they hid. He wasn't one of the those overtly muscular men whom she found such a turn-off, yet somehow he gave an impression of physical as well as mental power, of strength implicit in the long, lean lines of his body and limbs.

There was a collision of glances as she lifted her eyes to the idiosyncratic appeal of his dark face, and for several strangely mindless moments she was quite unable to look away. With her gaze locked to Rob's like this, she was prey to an odd prickly heat that was more internal than outward.

Then Rob stirred, and she was free, capable of thought again, and putting that heat down to embarrassment. This man knew too much about her; he knew the worst—that another man had rejected her and that she hadn't taken it as well as dignity demanded.

He was saying tauntingly, 'Insensitive, if you like, but still capable of much more real feeling than you are, I suspect, which is another reason I doubt whether what Olivier has done has truly left you devasted.'

'You're so clever, aren't you?' Lucia mocked, discovering that she didn't want Thierry to be a subject in this exchange—didn't want to talk or think about him ever again. 'Able to sum people up at a glance. Wouldn't it be nice if we could all do that instead of having to work at understanding people and then usually getting it wrong and being disappointed?'

'It didn't even take a glance,' he claimed with outrageous arrogance. 'I knew that about you before I set eyes on you. . . What have you got there?'

He was looking at her hands, which she held in front of her, the tense fingers playing nervously with the humble black and white shell she had picked up. Reluctantly she uncurled them to show him.

'It's a kind of periwinkle,' she vouchsafed.

'I know.' He sounded slightly surprised. 'No cowries this morning? They are usually a lot—unbroken too.'

He indicated the wavy, shining line where the sea had strewn its haphazard bounty, and Lucia shrugged self-consciously.

'Yes, I saw a few, but I used to call these luckies when I was small. I don't know where the idea came from; my mother probably. She used to tease my father by refusing to call things by their correct names. . .' Falling silent momentarily, she threw a defiant little smile up at him. 'Well, I need some luck, don't you think?'

Rob didn't respond immediately, scrutinising her upturned face reflectively before laughing. 'That's not a very scientific attitude, considering what you are.' The amusement receded. 'But we're both out of luck, Lucia. My sister wasn't exactly happy about your arrival, especially as Olivier is still so defensively vague about you.

'I did some deliberate misleading to the effect that by some impossible coincidence I'd met you in South Africa and we'd been attracted, so I don't want her getting hold of any idea that you might be languishing after Olivier or planning to win him back. . . So you and I are going to have to be seen to spend some time in each other's company while we're both here. The occasional meal together should do it.'

'Do you really expect me to care about your sister's feelings?' Lucia demanded indignantly. 'Forget it, Rob! I wasn't thinking properly yesterday, when I went along with that ridiculous fiction, but I want nothing more to do with it. I don't need it!'

'Are you sure of that?' he returned smoothly. 'You care about what people think of you or you wouldn't have made use of the face-saver I offered you for as much as a minute. You didn't want people knowing your pride was hurt. But this isn't for you; it's for Nadine—'

'No way—'

'Wait until I've finished, please,' he cut in, hard-faced now. 'I'm not wasting time using persuasion on someone as cussed as you, so here's the deal: I've said I don't interfere with the hiring and firing at my hotels, but in this case I'm willing to break my rule because I have a personal interest in doing so. Play this thing out, and properly—no giving the game away—or I will instruct Chester Watson to think again about the position he has for you.'

Lucia shot him a furiously resentful glance but remained silent, her fingers busy with the shell again. This was blackmail, and the thought of giving in to it made her blood boil, but did she have any choice? She needed a job, and urgently. Chester Watson thought that he had one for her here. Looking elsewhere might take time that she couldn't afford. So she couldn't afford pride either. She had to be practical.

'Couldn't you have thought of something that didn't involve our having to spend time together?' she asked resentfully, leaving her submission merely implied, since there was always the possibility that she might yet find a way of thwarting him.

'Something involving less intimacy? I wish!' he admitted feelingly. 'But what? Anyway, it's too late to change our story now.'

'And the whole thing is full of pitfalls,' she went on critically. 'Think of all the traps waiting for us, especially as we don't know a thing about each other—even if you do believe you've got me taped. I don't even know when you were in Johannesburg.'

'Neither does anyone else, and who is going to be so crude as to interrogate us about our relationship?' Rob was impatiently dismissive. 'If anyone is so crass, you can imitate Olivier's example and be vague—or coy if you think it's more appropriate. I don't go around discussing my affairs with people, and that includes Nadine, but we can exchange a few facts over dinner at one of the hotel restaurants tonight if you're worried about it. Agreed?'

'Your affairs,' Lucia echoed slowly, unexpectedly disturbed by the thought that occurred to her as she looked at him standing there, so emphatically masculine. 'Aren't they usually rather physical?'

He laughed with real amusement. 'Not necessarily immediately so. I usually take a little time to court my way into a woman's bed.'

'Really?' she snapped, that inner disturbance only increasing in response to his words. 'I wouldn't have thought someone so insensitive had that much finesse—or is it to give yourself a chance to back out if you discover something you don't like?'

Rob's eyes had hardened and his lips curled contemptuously.

'Why not? I don't squander myself on just anyone, but I also happen to have enough respect and liking for real, warm-blooded women to play things their way, and to enjoy doing so.'

The clear implication being that he didn't consider *her* a real, warm-blooded woman. Lucia's chin lifted.

'You— Oh, here we go!'

It was a typical island squall, with some clouds gathered overhead flinging down a soft scatter of warm tropical rain, although the sun still shone brilliantly, turning the drops a dazzling silver, the erratically gusting breeze alternatively swirling and slanting them.

Lucia moved out from under the coconut palm, not wanting any dust washed down onto her, and Rob did likewise but made no effort to head for proper cover, obviously as aware as she was that these showers frequently lasted no more than a few seconds.

'You seem to have some sort of a problem. Were you hoping I'd take you to bed to lend colour to our story or to salve your ego, now that Olivier no longer wants you? Forget it, Lucia; I'm not interested,' he stated bluntly, amusement indenting the corners of his mouth as he noted the glaze of anger in her eyes.

'Although I suppose a simple kiss wouldn't do any harm, especially now that we've got a potential audience. One or two people are beginning to appear, mostly out on their balconies, looking at the rain.'

'That's not necessary,' she snapped, with a little surge of alarm, seeing that he was suddenly closer to her. 'They're hotel guests; they don't know us, so what purpose can it serve?'

'A fair percentage will know who I am.' It wasn't conceited, merely a statement of fact. 'We establish ourselves as a couple, their acceptance of our relationship gets passed around in the course of casual conversation, and eventually it reaches the ears of those who count in this.'

'Dear Nadine,' Lucia supplied bitterly.

Rob didn't deny it. 'For Nadine to be convinced, the belief needs to be widespread.'

He was reaching for her. Her instinct was to back away, but she was not conscious of the figures up on the balconies of the sea-facing side of the hotel, which was situated on a slight rise of ground just above the beach, and, remembering his threat, she forced herself to stand still.

'I don't think I am going to like this,' she muttered tensely as she felt his hands on her shoulders gathering her close.

'I'm not doing it for pleasure either, darling, believe me,' he countered emphatically.

Now his arms were around her. Looking up into the dark, quirkily attractive face, Lucia pressed her lips firmly together, and he laughed.

He was so tall that he seemed to loom and hover over her, like some raptor over its prey, and she was transfixed by a sense of being under threat, or in a trap from which there was no escape.

Resentment followed swiftly in the wake of those moments of vulnerability. She resented so much—his height, the strength in the arms that held her, the news that he had given her yesterday and the situation he had created because of it, the need to spend even a minute in his company and, most of all, his general attitude allied to the humiliating things he knew about her.

So much of the anger she had been feeling since yesterday afternoon seemed to have been provoked by this man, rather than by what Thierry had done. She was angry again now, taut and shaking with rage at the position in which she found herself.

Determinedly she continued to keep her lips together as Rob's mouth covered hers, although the arrow of sensation that went shafting through her in the first few moments of contact caught her by surprise. Then she reminded herself that this was an act, essentially a display, and not intended for her benefit, let alone her enjoyment. Resolutely Lucia turned herself into a statue.

It was still raining slightly in soft, slanting drifts, and

Rob's shirt was as damp as hers. The shell had fallen from her hands just before they'd become trapped between their bodies, and now her palms were flattened against his chest.

With some idea of decreasing the intimacy of the embrace by holding him away, she slid her hands up to his strong shoulders. It proved to be a mistake. He simply gathered her closer, and now her breasts were pressed against the hardness of his chest and responding in their own special way to the tantalisation of his body-warmth.

That involuntary reaction persuaded her that it was time to end this. Rob's mouth was still moving on hers in a leisurely, thoughtful way that was almost lazy, as if he was both unsurprised and unperturbed by the continuing stiffness of her lips.

Afterwards Lucia couldn't be sure which had been responsible for defeating her resistance—that idly sensual mouth, the long fingers that strayed indolently up over her back to play lightly, teasingly about her shoulderblades and the nape of her neck, or simply the rain-dampened heat of his body.

Whatever it was, she was abruptly no longer proof against the pleasure of being in physical contact with such a magnificently made male. Her lips softened and parted, and the fingers that had been biting into his shoulders now unflexed and shaped themselves compliantly to their powerful curve.

Rob evinced no surprise at the change, merely accepting the invitation with facility and skill. A tiny sound of sheer unthinking relief escaped Lucia as she yielded to the slickly confident exploration he was making, her own lips and tongue beginning to stir in languorous co-operation with his caressingly probing tongue. It was as if every nerve-end in her mouth was suddenly acutely sensitised, making her physically aware of every minute sensation that accompanied this erotic, oddly searching kiss.

But as the rain ceased so did the kiss. When Rob released her she took a couple of steps back, slanting him a warily wondering look from beneath her eyelashes. Did he know that she had—felt something? She didn't want him to, but he probably did as it was blatantly obvious that he was both very skilled and very experienced with women.

'Not bad,' he commented judicially, regarding her in a disconcertingly speculative way. 'From a distance, it should have appeared suitably fervent.'

'I'd like it if *you* were at a distance,' she flared, determined not to let him know how shaken she was by those moments of weakness. 'Preferably the distance between continents.'

He laughed. 'What else, from someone as cold as you are? Although I have to say it goes somewhat strangely with all that red-hot rage you're wasting so much energy on.'

So perhaps he hadn't registered the fleeting pleasure she had taken from his mouth—although a certain glint in the smoky eyes warned her against being complacent. Nevertheless, Lucia knew a prick of chagrin at being called cold, because she knew she wasn't.

'Sorry if you're disappointed, but don't take it as a reflection on your expertise,' she offered in mock-consolation. 'I just don't like blackmailers. Anyway, I'm through with pleasing men.'

'"Pleasing men"?' Rob repeated with amused scepticism. 'Have you ever bothered much?'

'Too much,' she asserted feelingly.

Of course, he was probably talking in a purely sexual context, but it had just occurred to her that all her present troubles were the direct result of her desire to please those men she loved.

If her father hadn't been so anxious for her to get

her degree in marine biology, Thierry wouldn't have been left alone to find someone new. And hadn't she come back to the Comoros all set to please Thierry by staying at home on the estate once she was his wife, at the expense of her own inclination which was to go out to work in some job that involved meeting and dealing with people?

She had longed for a permanent home, but a home shouldn't be a prison. She had even been prepared to give serious consideration to his wish to start a family within the first year of marriage because she'd wanted to make up for his having to wait so long for her, although she really considered herself a year or two too young for motherhood.

Well, all that was over. She was free. Then the blaze of emotion faded from her heart-shaped face. She was free, but alone; her father and Thierry were both gone from her, and she had loved them. But one thing was for sure: no other man was going to do what Thierry had done to her. She wasn't giving him the opportunity.

'Too much by your own ungenerous standards, perhaps,' Rob was conceding, studying her face assessingly for a moment before letting his gaze sweep over her shirt, the gleam in his eyes becoming more pronounced. 'That shirt isn't serving much purpose.'

Soaked by the rain, it was now plastered to her, the thin black cotton semi-transparent where it clung to her body, shoulders and upper thighs.

'Neither is yours,' she retorted resentfully, removing hers and holding it out to dry in the brilliantly blazing sun.

Rob's shirt was similarly soaked, and there was something disturbing to her senses about the evidence of dark body-hair filling in a V across his upper chest and arrowing down to his waist. It was a mercy—or a pity, depending on your point of view—that his tough jeans hadn't also been rendered transparent.

With another man, under other circumstances, Lucia might have voiced the mischievous thought, but that it should pop into her mind so naughtily with regard to this man was infuriating, because she didn't want to be aware of him as male—virile and sexy.

'Why are you so angry about it?' he asked in a tone that suggested he knew very well. 'But then, everything makes you angry.'

'*You* do,' she emphasised incautiously.

'Ah, yes, still wanting to kill the messenger.' Rob shook his head in mock-disbelief. 'It's beyond me how Hassan Mohammed could have described you as sunny-natured. Unless he's seeing only what he wants to see, he can't know you very well.'

'Better than you do, anyway,' she asserted. 'I'm off. I want to shower and find out when Chester Watson can see me before I have breakfast—Oh! You've still got my engagement ring.'

On the point of departing, she swung round to face Rob again as she remembered. The expression of enjoyment had disappeared, leaving his face hard, and there was something relentless about the mouth which such a short while ago she would reluctantly have had to describe as sensual.

'As you're no longer engaged, the adjective doesn't apply, and whether it's your ring or Olivier's is debatable.'

'Oh, let's be precise by all means! Since neither Thierry nor I have actually broken off the engagement, it's still an engagement ring,' Lucia argued bitingly.

'What do you suppose he was doing yesterday, getting engaged to Nadine?' Rob enquired mildly, and shrugged. 'The ring is quite safe, Lucia.'

'I want it.'

'You can get it when we have dinner tonight. I'll have to let you know exactly when later, as I'm not only here to celebrate my sister's engagement and I'm not sure yet how my time will be taken up by the business side of things.'

She hesitated before accepting grudgingly. 'All right.'

As she turned and began to walk towards the hotel, the long, graceful curve of which copied the line of the beach, Rob fell into step beside her.

'Still intent on selling it?' he prompted.

'I might,' she said shortly; she knew that she would have to return it to Thierry, even if its cash value turned out to be the only thing between her and starvation, but she wasn't about to admit anything to this man.

'Because you're broke, aren't you, Lucia?' he prompted lightly. 'That's why you've decided to co-operate with me, isn't it? You really need that job.'

She stopped walking and flung him a furiously resentful look.

'You must be the most incredibly unpopular man! I hate people who know everything, and so does everyone else I know. Yes, I'm broke, and yes, that's the only reason I'm allowing you to blackmail me!' she conceded defiantly as he, too, halted.

'Why shouldn't I be? My father was only famous, not rich. When he died there was just enough money to cover my university fees and for my mother to go home to England and set up house with her divorced sister—although I think that arrangement is about to end as they're both seeing new men.

'I just hope that my mother's with someone settled this time, because she didn't really enjoy being itinerant. She used up all her emotional energy pretending she didn't mind and keeping my father happy. I suppose that's why I don't feel I know her. There was nothing left over for me.'

But rattling on like that failed to distract Rob from the relevant point. 'How have you managed trips back to the Comoros, or did Olivier finance them?'

'No. He couldn't. Just about everything the ylang-ylang brings in goes back into the estate. I worked nights and weekends—restaurants and a chain store—but what I made only stretched to the long vacs, except once when the South Africans were going through one of their optimistic periods and started going out a lot and tipping generously for a few months.'

'But this time you don't have a return ticket?'

Lucia winced secretly, because the stark fact said everything about the unwarranted complacency with which she had returned, all untroubled by any inkling of what might be awaiting her.

'So, you see, I'm really going to need that ring if Chester Watson doesn't come up with a job for me and I have difficulty finding something else,' she offered rebelliously. 'Or if I decide not to let you blackmail me after all.'

Rob shrugged as they resumed walking, obviously confident that he had already won and therefore indifferent to the threat.

'He seemed to think you were suitable for whatever he has in mind. I don't know what it is. As I say, I don't usually interfere with the human resources side of things unless it's vital—as now. It would undermine the confidence of those I employ to recruit personnel. . .

'It seems we have something in common. I too suffer from a parent who has found fame without much fortune. Jacynth Cole-Ballard,' he elaborated as Lucia shot him a questioning glance. 'And she's only famous among those who are interested in her subject.'

'The palaeoanthropologist!' Lucia was excited, her antagonism forgotten for the moment. 'I've read some of her books. She makes it all sound so fascinating, and I know she has done a lot to reconcile her discipline's findings with those of the DNA theorists. She made one of the important Kenyan discoveries, didn't she?'

The interest she felt made her light greeny-blue eyes

very clear and shining, and there was something thoughtful about the slight smile Rob gave her.

'Yes, she worked there a lot in the early years of her career. I think she's in Java these days, when she's not doing lecture tours.'

'What's she like?'

'You probably know as much as I do. I sometimes wonder if I'd recognise her if I encountered her unexpectedly.' He laughed suddenly. 'Thank you, Lucia, you've provided me with a novel experience. It doesn't usually require mention of my mother for me to impress a woman.'

Lucia regarded him warily, perplexed by the contradictory way in which his words could seem to indicate either sheer arrogance or an engaging self-mockery.

She shrugged. 'I'm not really impressed.'

But her curiosity was aroused, especially as she recalled that he had claimed to *suffer* from his famous parent.

'Then it's just as well I don't feel any burning need to impress you, isn't it?' Rob returned easily as they reached one of the entrances to the hotel. 'What I'd really like from you is your immediate departure from these islands, so you don't *have* to submit to blackmail, Lucia. You can leave at my expense. We can make it a loan or a gift, just as you prefer.'

Outrage jerked her head up and her sensitive mouth tightened as she stared at him with blazing eyes.

'You're really desperate to get rid of me, aren't you?' she accused. 'But you can forget it! I don't need any help from you, Rob.'

'What you mean is you're not prepared to accept any financial help from me,' he corrected her contemptuously, obviously unsurprised by her outburst. 'A bit of face-saving was another matter, wasn't it?'

'You weren't doing that for me.'

'No, but it benefited you,' Rob observed with cool

derision. 'All right, that's why I resorted to blackmail before making this offer—I guessed someone as bloody-minded as you would refuse it, even if it meant doing yourself down by delaying the start of the career for which you're trained. So just keep away from Thierry Olivier, Lucia. I warn you, I'll be watching you. I must go. I'll see you tonight.'

He left her seething. He was insufferable, and if only she possessed the necessary funds she would be off this island like a shot!

Or would she? She was conscious of an angry need to prove something to Rob Ballard, but precisely what she wanted to prove was obscure—perhaps that she was worth more than Thierry's rejection would seem to suggest. But that would mean winning Thierry back, and she definitely didn't want him back, she had decided.

Impatient with herself for allowing Rob to trouble her thoughts and emotions for as much as a second, Lucia made a determined effort to shut him out of her mind. She had more important things to concern her, such as her need for employment.

When she saw him a little later, Chester Watson listened courteously as she described her experience waiting tables and working tills; he then proceeded to outline the job that he was offering her—on the strength of her local reputation, it seemed.

It called for specialised skills, and Lucia possessed them to a degree that made her confident that she could compete with anyone anywhere. Nevertheless, it wasn't a job that she would have chosen for herself, but she was in no position to turn it down, and at least it had one enjoyable aspect in that it would bring her into contact with hotel guests.

'Your familiarity with these waters specifically and things marine generally will be a definite plus,' he told her. 'The young man I was thinking of hiring wouldn't have been nearly as knowledgeable—a marooned yachtsman.'

And, in his way, probably as desperately in need of employment as she was, Lucia reflected guiltily, remembering how frequently yachtsmen were stranded on these islands here in the mouth of the Mozambique Channel between Madagascar and the African mainland, their yachts generally requiring expensive repairs if they hadn't been lost altogether.

But she couldn't afford to make any altruistic gestures, so she smiled at Chester. 'I'll need a timetable of the tides and I want to inspect the underwater gear— and talk to the boatman as well,' she requested.

'Who, like so many people who are at home *on* the sea, is useless *in* it; he can't swim a stroke,' Chester laughed. 'I must organise a permit for you too. The equipment should meet with your approval as our contract is with one of the most reputable manufacturers in the world. Then, when you're satisfied and have worked out at what hours you'll be going out, I'll have notices put up and placed in the rooms, announcing this new service to our guests.'

'Don't just aim it at the action-orientated types, though,' Lucia suggested. 'Some people who aren't adrenalin-junkies might like the idea of a day on the water but won't want to do anything too physical, so make it clear that the diving and snorkelling are optional. That way we won't lose custom by the less adventurous members of parties or halves of couples persuading the others to give it a miss. People don't like being separated on holiday.'

'You're right,' Chester agreed. 'And I'm reassured. Obviously your proficiency in the water hasn't made you intolerant of those less skilled or daring.'

Lucia merely smiled, not about to tell him how truly

unadventurous she really was. She could do the job.
She didn't have to enjoy it.

She spent the next couple of hours diligently inspecting the hotel's diving equipment and then interviewing
the boatman—a local with the sort of mixed ancestry
that made him the indigenous version of Creole, who
was delighted at the prospect of this new venture
supplementing the income he earned taking the
occasional guests out fishing.

The Japanese-manufactured boat was of an unusual
design but familiar to her as it was widely used among
the islands—a solid, stable, diesel-fuelled craft with
outriggers and a double skin—virtually unsinkable.

Satisfied, she reported to Chester's assistant and was
directed to the room she was to occupy in the impressively comfortable, ground-floor staff quarters, where
she unpacked her belongings before going to lunch.

Conditions permitting, she planned to take her first
group out the following day, so the notices had gone
up by now, mentioning her name, and Hassan
Mohammed told her that there had already been
several enquiries and one definite booking.

Later in the afternoon she discovered that someone
must have pointed her out to interested guests, as first
she was waylaid by a group of teenage boys, one of
whom was a scholarly individual acquainted with her
father's work, and the rest of whom wanted to know
what sort of action they could expect if they joined one
of the outings.

Next came two couples—Senegalese and Austrian,
which wasn't unusual as most visitors to the Comoros
came from South Africa, the continent's several
French-speaking countries, or mainland Europe—
especially France.

Chester had told her that her job placed her loosely
among the hospitality and entertainment staff, where
socialising with guests was not only permitted but

encouraged if they showed an inclination that way. Thus Lucia accepted happily when the four invited her to join them for a sundowner in one of the alfresco bars, reflecting once more that this was the part of her job that she was going to enjoy.

It would be fun working for an establishment whose main aim was to please people, because that was what she was good at and liked doing, when she wasn't in the grip of rage and humiliation. She had always been a sociable person, getting a buzz out of meeting and mixing, and was lucky enough to get on well with most people.

She had just finished her drink and was drawing fascinated questions from her companions with the tale of an unfortunate swordfish that she had once seen caught here when her eyes encountered a shining red-gold head, and she hesitated momentarily.

The bar was thatched but open to the air on three sides, and Thierry was hovering on the outskirts, an unhappy look on his face.

Lucia finished her story and answered a few more questions before excusing herself. She knew Thierry must be looking for her and her first angry impulse was to refuse to have anything to do with him, but she also knew how much it would have cost him to overcome his natural inclination to avoid possible unpleasantness and seek her out.

For both their sakes this confrontation needed to be private, so, ensuring that Thierry had seen her, Lucia left the bar, finding a deserted bench above the beach and sitting down to wait for him.

CHAPTER FOUR

'AND SO, Thierry?'

It had taken Thierry a few minutes to follow her—regathering his courage, Lucia guessed—but now he stood in front of her in the softly golden light of a Comorean evening.

Lucia remained seated on the bench, suppressing an urge to leap up and hit him, and with no right any longer to leap up and hug him.

Her tightly laced fingers the only outward indication of the angry tension that possessed her, she looked up at him. He was such a beautiful man, with his velvety brown eyes and sensitive features, and he wasn't hers any more. She still didn't belong anywhere. She swallowed, noting that he wore an expression of utmost misery, and she felt her anger receding as she registered all over again how much effort it must have cost him to come here to her.

She rewarded the effort with the tiniest of smiles, but it did nothing to soothe Thierry, as he merely looked even more abject, and confused too, she observed.

'Lucia, what were you doing with Rob Ballard yesterday?' The first accusingly wounded question confirmed his state of mind. 'He says you met in Johannesburg. You never told me.'

'Well, we haven't been in touch much lately, have we?' she countered evasively, only realising as she said it that she was going with the lie—for his sake and for her pride's too, quite apart from Rob's threat—but disinclined to let him get away without some sr reproach to his conscience. 'I could ask a sim question, Thierry. What were you doing with Nadine Ballard?'

'I know!' he acknowledged miserably, but with a faint, underlying note of resentment. 'I was going to telephone, or write... I wasn't expecting you so soon.'

'Perhaps you hoped I'd simply never come back,' Lucia suggested waspishly. 'That I'd forget you so you could forget me—although you don't seem to have had too much trouble there.'

'You were never here!' He had progressed to trying to justify his behaviour.

Lucia sighed, knowing him too well for surprise or indignation.

'You agreed to wait until I had my degree,' she reminded him.

'Maybe you made me. You were so insistent about your promise to your father,' he attacked sulkily. 'You wanted to wait, and my mother also thought it would be for the best if we didn't rush into marriage, so I went along.'

'I'll bet she did,' Lucia agreed tartly. 'Mamma is thrilled by your new engagement, isn't she?'

'It's better all round,' Thierry agreed, suddenly almost eager, appealing for her understanding. 'We both know she never liked you, and I was sorry for that, but maybe she saw something.. .knew we weren't right. But Lucia—'

He broke off in alarm as she stood up, suddenly ʌnpatient with the whole situation. She didn't want ᴛ be here with Thierry, exchanging reproaches, ᴀuse some of the things she was feeling were ᵖʳessingly wrong, inappropriate to a broken heart. ᵧyway, he was part of her old life and she wanted to ᴀrt living the new one right now. Lucia gave him a ᴅde smile.

'It's all right, Thierry! Of course, you should have let

me know what was happening to you. . .' She heard
herself with distaste, because enough had already been
said; despite his attempts to turn this round and blame
her, his conscience was troubling him. 'But, thanks to
the craziest coincidence, we're both going to come out
of it all nicely undamaged. And if you really love
Nadine and think you'll be happy with her, then I do
wish you well.'

Thierry looked only half-relieved. 'Lucia, are you
sure? Do you really. . .? Is it all right?'

A certain degree of wistfulness lay in the brown eyes
as he stared at her, so slender in her white cotton shirt
and pink shorts which were subtly gathered to make
her waist look incredibly small, and Lucia kept on
smiling encouragingly.

'It really is,' she offered gently, lifting a hand to
his shoulder and giving it a reassuringly friendly
squeeze.

It was the wrong shoulder. The strangeness of the
idea disconcerted Lucia, especially as the sensation she
had was sufficiently powerful to make this idea almost
a conviction. Thierry's shoulder felt wrong to her hand
because her hand had recently rested on a harder,
stronger shoulder—Rob Ballard's, this morning, she
realised, with a little spurt of angry resentment after a
second or two.

'I'm glad—' Looking past her, Thierry broke off, his
expression grown discomfited as he moved out of her
reach. 'I ought to be going—Nadine will be
wondering. . .'

The excuse fading away into silence, he didn't even
wait for her response but departed abruptly.

The light had deepened to an amber glow and Lucia
let him go with a shrug and a breath of impatient
laughter. She stood staring unseeingly out to sea for a
few moments, registering and trying to analyse what
she was feeling now, in the aftermath of the encounter,

and discovering that she had spoken with some sincerity in wishing Thierry well.

Why not? After all, she had loved him. She still did, she supposed, although she hadn't expected a broken heart to feel quite like this. She felt more adrift than properly hurt, and her emotions had a lot to do with the need to relinquish the prospect of finally putting down roots, which had kept her going through the last three years.

There was so much anger involved too—a churning, boiling cauldron of it—and yet so little of it was truly directed at Thierry, or even at Nadine. Rob Ballard was its main target, or so it seemed. But wasn't it really aimed at her own folly, the way she had made a victim of herself with her loving desire to please the men in her life? And she had put her father before Thierry, which was why she had lost Thierry.

And she had been guilty of something similar just now, she acknowledged angrily. Stupid! Making it easy for Thierry, letting him get away with what he had done like that, still putting herself out, still denying her personal urges in order to please! Never again, not for anyone! Then she would never have to feel like this again.

As she swung round her breath caught in her throat and her heart gave a little jump of fright. Rob Ballard was standing on the slope above the bench, as dark as the long shadow he cast in this light, and something about his absolute stillness struck her as peculiarly threatening.

Then she expelled the arrested breath in a rush, almost glad to see him because here was a proper and worthy focus for her rage.

'Are you safe to approach?' he enquired amusedly, stirring and beginning to stroll towards her. 'You look so very furious... I trust that little scene wasn't the first shot of a campaign to win Olivier back, Lucia.'

'I didn't get time. You frightened him away.' She answered flippantly, with her best smile, as she guessed that he must have been responsible for Thierry's retreat.

'Yes, I suspect he thinks I've turned against him since I questioned him about you, and he's off to reassure Nadine in case I should report his lapse. To do him justice, I believe that's all it was—because he knows now that you're bad for him, so the reassurance will be genuine.

'In fact, I'm satisfied that he'll be good for her. He's just what she needs, even if he isn't the most exciting personality I've ever encountered. And it's only around you that he becomes a wimp. As I say, he knows it too, and he's ashamed. Letting himself become attracted to Nadine was the start of his fight against your influence.'

'You don't understand him!'

She was defensive, furious with herself for her quip because, of course, it had been a betrayal of Thierry, just as recalling the feel of Rob's shoulder had been. Then a fleeting look of confusion passed over her heart-shaped face because she no longer owed Thierry any loyalty, and the realisation engendered an anchorless feeling incongruously mixed with relief, or, perhaps, a sense of freedom—yet another betrayal, and this man's fault.

'What is there to understand? He isn't exactly complicated, but, as it happens, I do understand him. If I didn't, don't you think I'd be doing my utmost to dissuade my sister from marrying him?' Rob demanded.

'Oh, and I understand you too, Lucia. I understand why you believe such a man would suit you. It's the particular mix of your two personalities, what he becomes in response to you. You can push him around, force him to fall in with your plans.'

Lucia regarded him inimically, resenting the uncomfortable sensation that the words induced. Hadn't Thierry himself just virtually accused her of forcing him to accept a long engagement against his will? And she had known him well enough to be aware that he would offer little or no resistance rather than risk the disturbance of an argumentative confrontation.

She shrugged defiantly. 'Maybe that would suit *him*.'

'Too much of it would destroy him. Keep away from him, Lucia—especially if you have any genuine feeling for him. You're bad for him.'

His expression held her silent for a second. It was so strange—the way his mouth would seem so overtly sensual at some moments and utterly ruthless at others, as now. A frisson of apprehension shook her inwardly. You could never push this man around. He was too much the dominant, demanding male, and the reverse would be true: you could end up doing things against your will just because he had decided you should.

This uneasy recognition of his maleness and the powers it implied seemed to come from such a primitive part of her femininity that Lucia was incensed.

'I can't keep away—not yet, anyway,' she pointed out. 'Because you've still got my ring if I want to return it to him.'

'Ah, you've given up the idea of selling it?' In the gathering dusk his teeth looked very white as he smiled.

'I have a job now,' she admitted shortly.

'I've heard,' he acknowledged, 'and you know what you have to do to keep it. I'll let you have the ring tonight. That's why I was looking for you. Is dinner at eight all right?'

'I suppose, if we have to carry on with this nonsense,'

she agreed grudgingly, continuing rebelliously as she remembered, 'I let Thierry believe it.'

'Hoping to make him jealous?' Rob challenged softly. 'The look he gave me as he passed was somewhat resentful, now I think of it. Just remember that this charade isn't for your benefit, Lucia.'

'Nadine's,' she conceded bitterly, stirring. 'I'm going in.'

'Shall I come and fetch you later?'

'No, I'll meet you,' she snapped. 'Where?'

He told her, sounding amused now by her hostile attitude, but Lucia was in no mood to stay and give vent to her annoyance, turning and stalking away with only a brief nod of acknowledgement.

Rob Ballard was just too knowing, and too inclined to mock what he knew. Lucia loathed the thought of having to spend part of the evening in his company, but he was quite capable of telling Chester to find someone else to do her job if she refused to go along with the pretence he had devised.

When she had reached her room Madelon Brouard looked in to welcome her.

'I am going to Moroni for the evening, but I think you will have something arranged with Rob?' she guessed.

'Dinner,' Lucia confirmed.

'Lucky Lucia! And it is the sweet, early stage of not really knowing, am I right?' Madelon gestured expressively. 'Or you would not be in here, but sharing his suite. That liberates me. I need not have scruples. I should warn you that I made my—*opening move* when I encountered him this afternoon. He was friendly, possibly even flirtatious.'

'You're serious, aren't you?' Lucia prompted on a gasp of laughter.

'Serious in the way people are serious about sports—games! Love is a game. I like to compete, and I enjoy the victory too for a time. Then I seek another contest.'

She might suit Rob, Lucia reflected as Madelon departed, smiling happily. She suspected that he too only played at love. Had she been genuinely involved with him, she would have been uneasy. Madelon was so beautiful, and unexpectedly engaging in her outspokenness.

Shortly before eight she showered and put on one of the plain dresses which she knew suited her—short, straight and sleeveless, with a simple, round neckline, in a blue-green colour several shades deeper than her eyes. Her hair was due for a trim as soon as she could afford it, she reminded herself, feeling it swing against her shoulders after she had brushed it.

Lucia regarded her mirrored self with dislike, hating her mouth for the sensitivity it seemed to betray. Make-up might alter the impression but it would be a weakness, telling Rob Ballard and everyone else that she had something to hide, or that she cared.

He met her at the entrance to the restaurant he had chosen.

'Darling!'

Before she could read his intention and dodge him, he had placed his long, lean hands lightly on her shoulders and was dipping his head to place a kiss at the corner of her mouth.

'No need to overdo it,' she snapped, stepping back smartly, and he gave her a challenging smile.

'Such a tame little kiss is hardly excessive to the impression we want to create. *Don't* rub it off,' he added sharply, catching hold of her wrist as she lifted her hand to do just that. 'What a baby! If you don't like it, it's your own fault, Lucia. If you'd agreed to let me fetch you from your room, people would just have had to assume a kiss of greeting, but meeting here necessitates the real thing.'

'What sacrifices you're ready to make for your sister,' she taunted, tugging her wrist free.

Her skin burned where his lips had rested, and her wrist still seemed to feel the circle of his fingers, her flesh strangely sensitised.

Sheer rage enabled her to smile brilliantly as the restaurant's deferential head waiter approached to show them to their table out on the balcony at the open end of the restaurant.

Lucia noticed the interest Rob attracted from most of the diners they passed, and she was aware of a fluttering alertness among the staff on duty, suggesting that his arrival had put them on their mettle. She wondered what it felt like to possess such powerful influence.

'Not such a sacrifice,' Rob contradicted her lazily when they were left alone, subjecting her to a leisurely but thorough appraisal. 'Physically you're a very attractive girl—which just makes all the other things you are even more of a pity.'

Lucia glared back at him. In his casual but classy clothes he really was devastatingly attractive in a unique, idiosyncratic way, and she recalled how sexy she had thought him for a few minutes the previous day, before he had grabbed her and told her what Thierry had done.

But it was something other than the outward appearance that disconcerted her. His personality was responsible, she supposed. It seemed to leap forward to meet her, filling the atmosphere with complex, silent vibrations, threatening to overwhelm.

'You don't know what I am.' Accepting a menu from another waiter, she gave it the briefest of glances before handing it back, saying decisively, 'I'll have prawns with a salad, no starter and nothing to drink first.'

'Wine with them?' Rob prompted as the wine-waiter arrived.

Lucia hesitated. 'All right, but I must limit myself to one glass. I'm diving tomorrow.'

'Chester Watson was telling me what you'll be doing,' Rob commented when they had finished ordering.

'Taking groups of guests out on a boat for part of a day, diving with them, instructing them if they haven't done it before. We're also offering snorkelling. The boatman wanted to include fishing, but I told him I'd rather he kept those trips separate from mine because I can't stand seeing the gaffing, and I'm sure some of the guests will feel the same.'

'And you're competent to undertake this sort of thing?' he asked inscrutably.

Lucia's chin rose. 'Yes.'

'I gather you have something of a local reputation. . . the island mermaid. What's wrong?' he added as she grimaced slightly and, seeing his gaze drop briefly to her hands which were playing nervously with her butter-knife, forced them to be still.

'Nothing, I was just thinking of the creature that must have given rise to the mermaid myths. The *lamantin*,' she prevaricated and, unsure if he knew French, translated, 'You know, the dugong or mantee.'

'Sirenians. I know they're occasionally seen in these waters.'

'I've seen one. The poor thing was so ugly.' Sympathy made her voice tender. 'But they really do have breasts and hold their young in the forelimbs when they're suckling, just like a human mother.'

'Or any primate, according to an ex-girlfriend of mine who worked with chimpanzees and gorillas.' The laughter that lit Rob's dark face added a new dimension to his appeal. 'I suppose after the long months sailors used to have to spend at sea without sight of a woman anything remotely resembling one looked ravishing, hence the legends.'

'Men being what they are,' she agreed laughingly, hostility fleetingly forgotten in the moment of shared humour.

'But you don't like being called a mermaid?'

The personal note restored resentment and she was glad of it. She didn't want to like him—didn't want to be charmed. She shrugged.

'I don't care. It's meant as a compliment. I'm good in the water.'

'You'd better be,' he cautioned her. 'The Ballard Group isn't a charity.'

'And I'm not a charity case,' she asserted stiffly.

'Just desperately in need of a job. You'll need a permit.'

'Chester Watson is seeing to it.'

'He said. He didn't seem to think there'd be any trouble, especially if he told the authorities whose daughter you are.' Seeing her head jerk up and the colour that touched her cheeks, Rob smiled mockingly. 'Don't be so touchy about it. You can't afford pride when you're so in need.'

'I've got the job because of things I can do, not because of who my father was,' she snapped, although, as always, she was ruefully aware that she could only do those things because of her father. 'And I'm not touchy. I'm proud of my dad. I don't go around saying I *suffer* from a famous parent, like you did this morning.'

She had hoped to turn the tables by eliciting a defensive reaction from him, but he merely looked indolently amused.

'I was exaggerating. I don't think I've really suffered, but I have had to assume responsibilities that shouldn't

have been mine—such as bringing Nadine up, as our
father died when she was still a child and our mother
was permanently away working.'

Rob shrugged. 'She's brilliant at what she does, and
very dedicated—to the exclusion of having time for
family life. It's just remarkable that she ever got
married and had two kids, but the eight-year age-gap
between Nadine and me says a lot about how rarely
she feels able to take time off.'

Lucia was reluctantly intrigued, wondering if Jacynth
Cole-Ballard's obsessions with her work was responsible for his stated disinclination to get personally
involved with career women.

'Is it in reaction to her absences that neither you nor
your sister have followed her into palaeoanthropology,
then?' she asked directly.

'From my point of view, humankind's past is academ-
ically interesting but it's the future and the living that
really grab me, and you could say that the hotel
industry is in our blood, as our father had a small hotel
in Zimbabwe. He was from settler stock. He met our
mother when she came down to Harare from Kenya
and stayed there.'

Rob's face hardened. 'But yes, I would have to say
that I suspect she's the reason for Nadine's determination to be a wife and mother first and foremost.'

'And now she's going to be,' Lucia taunted, riled by
the need to acknowledge, albeit only in the secrecy of
her mind, that if those were Nadine's primary aims in
life then she would suit Thierry perfectly.

But *she* had suited him too!

'As long as you do nothing to stop it,' Rob agreed
sardonically, and it was as if he had read her thoughts,
because he went on mockingly, 'She'll suit Olivier
perfectly, won't she, Lucia?'

Her eyes blazed. 'I've suited him very well for the
last three years.'

'When you were around.'

'If you want me to go on playing this game for dear Nadine's sake, then you'll have to leave Thierry out of the conversation,' Lucia flared. 'You don't know anything about the relationship I had with him.'

'I know enough. But all right—I don't think I want to know more,' he conceded enigmatically, glancing once more at her hands which were betraying her again, twisting and turning, toying with the cutlery.

This was so difficult! Lucia expelled an angry sigh and gazed away out into the darkness, which was intermittently lit here and there with small, random swirls and streaks of light marking the haphazard, darting flights of fireflies.

Here she was in a perfumed tropical paradise, seated opposite an attractive, dynamic, intelligent and sexy man, with a feast of prawns about to be set before her, and all she could feel was rage.

'I've missed these,' she offered in an attempt at neutral conversation when the prawns arrived.

'I've always been able to order them in Johannesburg,' Rob said questioningly. 'Mozambiquean, usually, and not beyond the means of impoverished students.'

'They were the speciality of the last restaurant I worked at, but they're different here.'

He laughed. 'When Mozambique is just across the water? We're *in* the Mozambique Channel.'

'Comorean are different,' she insisted, and he laughed again. 'The best I've ever had were cooked over a wood fire.'

'Then we must attend one of the barbecue nights they have here.'

They were both adults after all, Lucia accepted, playing her part in keeping the impersonal conversation going as they ate. Forced into each other's alien company by both his concern for his sister and her fear of

losing the job she had been lucky to get, they ought to
have been able to refrain from letting their mutual
dislike dominate the situation.

Nevertheless, she remained inwardly tense, needing
her anger to keep on smiling and talking. Aware that
she was on show, and that word could get back to
Thierry, his mother and her various local acquaint-
ances, she knew that she had to sustain the act or face
humiliation.

The thought forced her to admit that this pretence
benefited her too, but she didn't want Rob knowing
that.

During the meal a few people came over to introduce
themselves to Rob—the sort of over-bold celebrity
collectors to whom it never occurred that public figures
were not necessarily also public property. Lucia had to
acknowledge that he dealt with them impressively,
getting rid of even the most thick-skinned with a
minimum of effort and yet with absolute charm, so that
they all went away without taking offence and most
probably feeling flattered.

'How do you stand it?' she asked.

'I don't have a choice. It goes with the territory.
What about some mango ice cream?' he added, seeing
that she had finished her prawns and was rinsing her
fingers in the bowl provided, refusing to be tempted by
a sumptuous selection of sweets. 'It would be appropriate to you—sweet and cold.'

'You don't know if I'm sweet or not!' For some
obscure reason Lucia felt indignant.

'Oh, I think you can be,' he stated confidently. 'I've
learnt a few more things about you this evening.'

'Like what?' she demanded, on the defensive now.

'For instance, there's the fact that you're kind
enough to feel sympathy for dumb creatures, such as
fish being gaffed and unprepossessing dugongs,' he
offered lazily, and she wondered if he saw it as a

weakness. 'Then, it's obvious that you know your own mind, or know what you want and won't be swayed—although whether what you want is always right for you is debatable, remembering your engagement to Olivier.'

'I've told you, I won't discuss him with you,' she snapped. 'And you can't know if I'm cold either.'

'I know.' He spoke with lazy arrogance.

'How, when you've only known me a little over twenty-four hours? No one who really knows me will have told you that. Not Hassan Mohammed—'

'Definitely not him. I've already commented on a certain blindness there, haven't I?'

'And not Thierry, because they know I'm not, and, anyway, it's rather obvious that you and Thierry haven't exactly got one of those close, buddy-buddy relationships, although I know how most men carry on, discussing women among themselves, rating them.'

'Don't women?' Rob retorted. 'And I thought you didn't want Olivier in the conversation? But at least men don't bitch about each other to the opposite sex. Women have been their own worst enemies in the sex war.'

'I'm not interested in sexual politics, but men only stick together so loyally because they're so insecure,' Lucia accused. 'And where did you get this idea that I'm cold? Just because I didn't kiss you back with the greatest enthusiasm this morning? Because, of course, it can't be you who failed there, so it must be me. I did tell you not to take it personally.'

She wasn't really sure if she wanted him to go on believing that she was cold or not.

'Because you're done with pleasing men?' he mocked, eyes beginning to sparkle with relish. 'But, in case you failed to notice this morning, I wasn't exactly putting much into it either. It was for show, remember. But I knew you were cold before I met you, Lucia.'

'Right!' She made up her mind. 'I'm cold and I didn't really love Thierry.'

'So wanting to get him back is pure pride,' Rob derided, 'and pride is a cold thing.'

'I don't want him back,' she claimed savagely.

'No, you don't want *him*, you want him *back*,' he said bitingly. 'For your pride's sake, not because you love him. Anger is the only real, warm emotion you're capable of feeling, isn't it? And it can be a destructive one.'

'I think I'm entitled to be angry right now, having to sit here listening to you claiming to know all about me when you don't really know the first thing,' she countered furiously, just managing an insouciant smile as a waiter arrived with their coffee.

'That's not all that's making you angry, though, is it?' Rob challenged softly.

'Can I have my ring, please?' she requested tautly, refusing to react directly.

'It's in the safe. We'll fetch it as soon as we've finished. But why is it so urgent? You haven't arranged to meet Olivier again tonight, have you?'

Lucia widened her eyes in response to the smoothly taunting tone. 'Does Nadine let him out on his own at night?'

'She'd be a fool if she did.'

'Now that I'm around?' she prompted caustically.

'You said it.' His tone was grim.

'Isn't she sure of him either?' she enquired sweetly. '*You* seem to think I'm a danger—that I could get him back.'

The idea was something of a balm to her ego.

'You're strong-willed, and Olivier becomes weak where you are concerned,' Rob responded flatly, but then his voice hardened as he added, 'Though I ought to warn you that if you're intent on fighting my sister for him you're likely to find that she has her own arsenal, and the weapons in it may well prove more subtly effective than yours, Lucia.'

So, it was what he saw as Thierry's reaction to her rather than any qualities she might possess that he regarded as a threat to his sister. Resolutely Lucia assumed a wooden expression.

Suddenly she felt drained, wanting the evening to be over, her ordeal at an end, but there was this man, and all those people seated at the other tables, to prevent her shoulders slumping.

It seemed an age before her coffee was cool enough to drink, and not for the first time she cursed the high boiling point found at sea level, having frequently scalded her mouth on her return trips from the high altitude of Johannesburg over the years.

Finally, though, they were leaving the restaurant.

'My ring,' Lucia reminded Rob tightly.

'Not the hotel safe; I've got a private one in my suite,' he said, seeing the direction in which she was turning and slanting her a smile of mock-sympathy as she regarded him questioningly. 'It does fit in well with our charade, as naturally we'd want some privacy. This way people can just assume any lovemaking.'

She shrugged. 'All right, but I'm not staying long enough for them to be able to assume any proper lovemaking.'

'They can assume this thing is still in its earliest, unconsummated stages,' he agreed calmly.

'"The sweet, early stage of not really knowing",' Lucia quoted, and explained, 'Madelon Brouard said that to me earlier.'

'She's an intelligent woman,' Rob commented appreciatively. 'Rushing headlong into an affair means you miss out on several highly enjoyable phases.'

She looked at him curiously. 'I suppose, if I hadn't

arrived and you hadn't decided to go in for this stupid pretence, you'd be—courting her?'

'It's possible,' he allowed very coolly. 'She has an appealing personality and she's very lovely.'

'Don't make it sound as if I'm putting you out! You were the one who decided on all this, not me, so I'm not doing any apologising.' Lucia flung him a blisteringly defiant smile. 'But I don't know how you expect this charade to stand up if you're going to go around flirting with Madelon half the time—which is how she interpreted whatever you said to her this afternoon. I'm playing my part, but you're not.'

Rob was looking amused. 'We're not pretending to be married, just courting, so there's nothing contradictory about my behaviour.'

'Oh, yes, I'm sure it's absolutely characteristic of you to be keeping your options open,' she condemned.

'Exactly!' He was smiling knowledgeably.

'Well, if you're interested in Madelon, why don't we decide we're incompatible right now, tonight? Then you'll be free.'

'And so will you—to go running after Thierry Olivier?' he guessed contemptuously. 'Sorry, Lucia, it's too soon yet, and I don't trust you.'

She curbed an impulse to hit out at him physically, determinedly maintaining her smile.

'Oh, I suppose I might be doing Madelon a favour by letting you blackmail me, as I don't think she knows what you're really like,' she mocked.

'Neither do you yet, lady.'

'Why shouldn't I, when you claim to know all about me on the strength of such a short acquaintance?' she countered tartly, but he merely laughed.

Usually Lucia would have given a great deal more careful consideration to the issue before agreeing to accompany a virtual stranger to his suite, but, as it was so obvious that Rob Ballard felt absolutely no sexual curiosity whatsoever about her, to have demurred would have been to make herself look and feel silly.

Thus she went with him, intent on taking her engagement ring and departing at once.

His suite was luxuriously comfortable but clearly used for work, one end of the spacious living area occupied by a large, angled desk specially designed for the computer and sophisticated accessories it accommodated.

Lucia heard Rob close the door and then went rigid with shock as she felt his hands on her shoulders, turning her to face him.

CHAPTER FIVE

'OH, YOU were dead right after all!' Lucia blazed at Rob, in an absolute rage with herself for having been so unsuspecting. 'I didn't know what you were like, or I wouldn't have come here with you, but I'm finding out now, aren't I? Get your hands off me.'

'Calm down; this isn't a pass.' Rob's voice carried an undercurrent of amusement. 'But I do want you to relax, Lucia—'

'How can I when you're—?'

'You're such a very angry young woman.' He cut into her furious protest as she twitched angrily beneath his hands, endeavouring to shrug them off. 'But you've been angry long enough. Drop it, give yourself a break, if only for now. You don't need all that rage here; you don't need it to keep going, keep up the act. We're alone. There's no one to see so you can let go.'

And she had nothing to hide from him.

'Because you already know it all, don't you?' she accused bitterly, thinking that she hated him most for the way he really did seem to know so much about her.

'All of it—the worst and the best,' Rob confirmed in a light murmur, his hands moving on her shoulders now, his long fingers investigating them with slow, gently massaging rhythm. 'So you don't need the anger here. Hell, it must exhaust you, keeping it up all the time. You're so tense... Relax, or you're not going to be fit to dive and take responsibility for amateurs diving tomorrow.'

'I'll relax when I'm shot of you,' she declared tightly, and clenched her teeth so that even her jaw was rigid as she steeled herself to withstand whatever it was his leisurely fingers were doing to her.

Why did he have to be right so often? She did feel exhausted, every muscle aching from the tension that had gripped her while she had been on view to the public.

And she was still on show now, to this man.

But why let it matter? As he had said, Rob really did know the worst of her, so there was no need to go on pretending. The acceptance brought an odd sensation of relief, although at some hypercritical level of her mind she suspected herself of weakness.

But he was responsible for the weakness. That was what those fingers were doing—working the weakness into her. And she was suddenly too tired to fight it, already drained of most of her resilience by all the emotional demands that she had been forced to meet since her arrival the previous day.

Rob's hands were at her back now, occasionally returning to her shoulders or straying up to her taut, slender neck beneath the straight, satin-smooth fall of her hair. Constantly on the move, gently kneading at sore, knotted muscles or massaging her stiff spine, his fingers engendered some kind of trance.

Lucia simply stood there, no longer thinking at all, unseeing eyes staring straight ahead at his throat, and she was unaware that her hands involuntarily lifted to his sides, remaining otherwise passive, the fingers loosely curled.

She had a sense of being eased, or soothed and comforted, and she wanted to close her eyes and go to sleep, or perhaps weep, but even those actions required too much effort so she went on standing there, letting him do what he would.

'Better,' Rob was observing in an hypnotic murmur. 'Much better, Lucia.'

Now, as if triggered by his voice, came a sensation of

letting go—mentally, emotionally and physically. Lucia went as limp as a puppet abandoned by the puppet-master, and Rob's strong, confident arms were there to catch her as she collapsed helplessly against him.

Their magic performed, his hands were still now as he held her, virtually supporting her, and her head found a secure resting place against the solid strength of his shoulder. Still mindless, and with her eyes closed at last, Lucia breathed in the subtle male scent of him and accepted his warmth, letting it seep into her to add a feeling of lethargic well-being to the soothing work his hands had done.

In drifting, dislocated fashion, she felt that perfection or perfect peace would be if Rob were seated, she cradled in his lap, only she didn't really want to have to move from where she was right now, even for a moment.

But after a while the quality of the embrace began to undergo a gradual, subtle alteration. Calmness was lost to awareness. Lucia experienced it first as an inner stirring putting slow flight to the emotional void that had been so briefly healing.

The stirring became a tingle, bringing an end to her surrender to the relief of absolute blankness.

'I. . .' Her voice sounded both muffled and faraway, and she let it go, unsure of what she wanted to say anyway.

'And who would have thought you could ever be so yielding when you've been so ultra-defensive until now?'

Rob's voice contained a note of amused incredulity, and she lifted her head to catch a glimpse of something similar in the smoky eyes—interest touched with amusement.

His face was so close—too close—so very dark and yet lit with a complicated enjoyment that served as a warning to her suddenly alert senses.

Rob gave her no opportunity to act on it, his mouth capturing the softness of her lips with devastatingly skilled assurance.

She knew a moment of shock, which gave way to sizzling rage at the way he was taking advantage of her weakness, but in the ensuing second that too was giving way—to a wholly different type of weakness, and incipient pleasure.

Lucia's hands flew to Rob's shoulders and clung as his lips brushed back and forth across hers, sensitising them incredibly, making her acutely aware of every slight sensation, though the pressure of his mouth remained light, its questing movement almost idly experimental.

Warmth swiftly became heat. She could feel it coursing through her body and burning her face as her mouth took fire from his—an intense, sparking conflagration. Of their own accord, her arms went round his powerful neck and her mouth was signalling its willingness to draw him in—an invitation he accepted with confident ease.

The sheer physical pleasure to be had from being in contact with such a beautifully constructed man made Lucia stir convulsively. In response Rob gathered her in still closer, and her leaping senses thrilled to the taut male strength of his body.

She made a sharp sound of involuntary protest as his mouth left hers, but in the next instant her feverishly seeking lips had found his again, and their mouths became a single, moist cavern of heated, swirling demand and response once more.

Now his hands were moving about her body again, only their task was no longer to soothe but to arouse with erotic, exploratory caresses, and Lucia moaned helplessly under the overwhelming force of the stinging delight they created.

She was tense and shaking with the passion he had

ignited, wanting more, to be closer still with nothing between them, to tear his clothes off and—

Perhaps it was the vision of herself doing just that which restored the capacity to think, and with it an awareness of reality: where she was, what she was doing, and who he and she were.

Then the heat flooding her face no longer had desire as its source. Rage and shame were responsible, because she knew that she had no one but herself to blame for her predicament. She had let this begin, had let him kiss her, and had responded to him.

With a tiny sound of acute distress she attempted to free her mouth, and for the briefest of moments Rob reacted by subjecting her to the full weight of an almost aching sensuality, deepening the kiss with a surging, thrusting movement, literally possessing her mouth, commanding it, while his body seemed to vibrate subtly against hers, exerting an intimate pressure.

But then the real desperation with which she tried to move her face to one side must have reached him through whatever it was that drove him, and he was freeing her.

Face flaming, eyes blazing, Lucia couldn't speak, too conscious of her own culpability—considering the positive role she had played in what had just occurred—to know quite how to attack him, although every angry instinct she owned was urging attack.

'That was—'

'You!' Fury made her incoherent when finally she found her voice. 'Taking advantage of me!'

Anger darkened Rob's face fleetingly, but it was banished by a subsequent expression of amusement flitting across his features and putting a gleam in the smoke-coloured eyes.

'Hardly, when I haven't taken you off to bed and have no intention of doing so,' he drawled. 'A couple of kisses, Lucia? For which I had your fullest co-operation, I might add.'

'And I'm ashamed!' she flared, unable to deny it.

'Why should you be ashamed of something as healthy and natural as frustration? Because let's assume that's what was behind your rather enthusiastic participation. You've been separated from Olivier a long time and now come back to find he's no longer yours.' Rob paused before asking abruptly, 'Were you faithful to him the whole time you were away at varsity?'

'Yes!' Fiercely, but with bitterness surfacing, she continued, 'Although I suppose you're like his mother! From something she said to me yesterday it's obvious that she thinks I've found all sorts of *distractions* for myself over the years.'

She had looked often, of course—as she had looked at him yesterday—and had enjoyed long, speculative discussions about various males with her friends, but she had never been even remotely tempted to find a temporary substitute for Thierry.

Rob was regarding her thoughtfully. 'No,' he eventually offered slowly. 'That intense pride of yours wouldn't allow you to be unfaithful. You'd have had too hard a time living with yourself afterwards; and you'd never let yourself in for the discomfort of despising yourself.'

'I'm doing it right now!' Lucia snapped, and his expression hardened.

'Why? Because you now feel as if you finally have been unfaithful to Olivier? But he doesn't want you any more, Lucia,' he reminded her brutally. 'So instead of all this self-disgust you should be directing your anger at him, as he's at least partly responsible for your frustration.'

'I am not frustrated!' Lucia's voice took an upward swoop.

Belatedly it occurred to her that it might be prefer-

able to have Rob believe that frustration really had
occasioned her response to him, but it was too late to
retract the declaration now, and anyway she knew that
frustration had nothing to do with what she had felt—
although what *had* been responsible remained a
mystery.

'Then what was going on, and why this excess of
shame?' Rob's eyes had narrowed, and although he
spoke softly there was something implacable colouring
his tone, causing Lucia a frisson of unease. 'Because
you ended up actually enjoying yourself when you'd
simply set out to try and prove you can still pull a man?
I'm not an ego-therapist, Lucia.'

'I don't need to prove anything to anyone!'

But she did—she did! Only how could she ever prove
anything worthwhile to this man? That was what was
causing this crushing shame. He had kissed her, presumably with some pleasure, or he would have stopped
what was happening much sooner, but how could he
ever respect her when he knew that a man had rejected
her and believed that she had brought it on herself by
her commitment to getting her degree? The idea of
having shared part of herself—if only her kisses—with
someone who must hold her in contempt was
anathema.

'But, for anything it's worth,' Rob was going on
musingly, 'you are very attractive—very lovely and
quite seductively responsive. All of which, as I've said
before, makes the other things you are a great pity. I
could wish you weren't. . .what you are.

'But it's just as well I'm not interested in entangling
my life with yours, because I suppose I'd have to
wonder if I'd caught you on the rebound when you've
been so delightfully responsive this soon after learning
you've lost Olivier.'

He frowned suddenly as he came to a halt, as if

arrested by some troublesome thought, and Lucia saw that his mouth had tightened.

'I'm not on the rebound,' she asserted stiffly. 'I don't care about Thierry.'

'And never really did.' His expression had cleared and laughter lurked in his voice. 'All right, Lucia, I've now offered you several excuses for your behaviour and you've rejected the lot of them, so you figure it out.'

That was just what she couldn't do. When she disliked and resented him so much, how could he have incited that swamping welter of passionate desire?

'My ring,' she reminded him tautly, 'and then I'm out of here.'

With a brief inclination of his head Rob moved away.

'Going to return it to Olivier?' he enquired casually as he dropped it into her palm a minute later.

'Probably,' she conceded reluctantly, and was incensed by his knowing smile. 'Why do you have to keep on calling him "Olivier" in that stupid, macho way? His name is Thierry and he is going to be your brother-in-law, after all.'

His laughter rang with genuine amusement at that. 'Ah, Lucia, anything for an argument. You really are the most quarrelsome person I've ever met. Come, I'll see you to your room; and don't bother trying to make a quarrel of that as well. We still have a show to present remember?'

'Why can't we have discovered we're incompatible?' she demanded resentfully as he held open the door for her. 'We *are*.'

'You're so right!' he replied emphatically. 'But I don't trust you yet, angel, especially now that you're in a rage again. It's almost perpetual, isn't it?'

In fact, she had experienced more rage between the previous afternoon and tonight than she had done in the rest of her life. Belatedly on her dignity, Lucia declined to respond.

When they reached the door to her room, he gave her a taunting smile.

'Luckily for us both, there's no one around, so it can finally be a real case of an assumed kiss. I'll see you tomorrow.'

'Not if I see you first,' Lucia muttered childishly, and was enraged all over again when he went away laughing.

She felt angry and confused, her bewilderment aggravated by her continuing inability to direct her anger properly at those primarily responsible for the intolerable situation in which she found herself—Thierry and Nadine Ballard. Rob remained the focus of most of it, save for a substantial portion reserved for herself.

For a while in bed she burned with embarrassment over the way she had responded to him tonight, before defiantly deciding that he really had taken advantage of her, because, of course, she hadn't been her usual self when he had first worked that trick with his hands, getting her to relax so completely, to let go of all the turbulent anger and pride which would normally have ensured her absolute resistance.

Then, a little surprisingly, she fell asleep, and slept well, and awoke looking forward to starting her job— or at least to the more enjoyable aspects of it, she acknowledged honestly.

One definite bonus of it lay in the fact that she would be free of Rob's infuriating presence for the bulk of the day—and she could guess how he would be spending it, she reflected tartly a little later, catching a glimpse of him standing talking to Madelon as she opened the hotel shop.

Instead of resenting the double standard which allowed him to make only a token contribution to the pretence he had decided was necessary, maybe she should be hoping that he would find Madelon so irresistible that he would decide he had no time to spare for a fake romance.

The party Lucia was to take out numbered six, she learnt from Hassan Mohammed, who had taken the bookings.

'That's not bad, considering the notices only went up yesterday. The boatman and I make eight, so we're only two short of the maximum the boat can comfortably take.'

Two staff members carried the refrigerated box containing lunch, and the diving and snorkelling equipment down to the arranged meeting place, and she could see Basile, the boatman, bringing his craft in to pick them up as she introduced herself to the three couples—from France, the Ivory Coast and South Africa—who made up the party.

She was answering some of their questions, telling them what they could expect from the day, and asking some of her own about their swimming abilities and diving experience when she saw Rob Ballard strolling down the beach towards them, clad in swimming trunks and a loose shirt.

'The name Comoros or Comores means the islands of the moon, but it's the sun we've got to worry about today, so I hope you've all got plenty of sunblock,' she told them, then repeated it in French, and added with a smile. 'Will you excuse me for a minute, please?'

She moved swiftly up the beach to intercept Rob, grateful for her concealing sunglasses in case her eyes betrayed how vividly she was suddenly recalling what had happened last night.

'You look the part, anyway,' he commented easily, observing the pareo she wore wound about her slim body, its soft white cotton printed with pale green sea-horses.

'You really are overdoing the act if you're pretending to be so crazy about me that you have to come and see me off to my day's work,' Lucia snapped, finding the sight of his long, deeply tanned legs disturbing.

'Not seeing you off, going with you,' he stated blandly.

'You are not!' she exploded.

'The devoted Hassan Mohammed tells me you've got the space,' he said, his tone still suspiciously neutral.

'The *treacherous* Hassan, in that case! That isn't just overdoing it, it's turning the whole thing into a farce— a caricature! You don't go and sit in your real girl-friends' offices, or wherever they work, all day, do you?'

'This isn't pleasure or even pretended pleasure but business of a kind, as I'm looking after the hotel's interests.' Rob paused deliberately. 'I want to be sure you know what you're doing. The Ballard Group isn't a charity.'

'You said you don't usually interfere with the hiring and firing, and the thing that might have made you break your rule—Nadine's peace of mind—isn't an issue here as she and Thierry aren't around!' she reminded him accusingly. 'What do you imagine I did? Flung myself at Chester's feet with such a good sob story that he acted unprofessionally and gave me this job without bothering to find out if I could do it?'

'I know you didn't, and I know he wouldn't,' he returned dismissively. 'Nevertheless, he hasn't seen what you can do. He has only heard about it. I want to see if you live up to your reputation.'

'No way—'

'You are currently employed by the Ballard Group, Lucia.' Rob was beginning to show signs of impatience.

'And you are Ballard,' Lucia acknowledged bitterly.

'The boss,' he agreed, with a significantly taunting smile.

She hesitated. She really needed this job, and she knew that she was capable of all that it required. Rob was probably hoping she wasn't, as his preferred solution to the situation created by Thierry and Nadine was obviously to have her off the island.

If she refused to co-operate with him now, she supposed that he could have her fired, and she wasn't sure how much influence such a man wielded—whether it was sufficiently far-reaching for him to be able to block any alternative employment she went after, or have her deported when she failed to find a job.

'Are you sure you can bear to tear youself away from Madelon?'

That amused him. 'Keep on sounding so jealous. It makes our act more convincing.'

'Your ear is at fault. It's pity you're hearing. I feel sorry for her! At least you're only pretending to be interested in me. All right, I know I can't stop you coming out with us,' she yielded tautly, 'but I don't want these people knowing you're checking up on me or their confidence in me will be destroyed.'

'We'll let them assume I can't bear to let you out of my sight.' Rob laughed as she opened her mouth to argue. 'Don't worry; I won't distract you with any overtly lover-like behaviour.'

He distracted her by existing, she reflected resentfully.

'Can you swim?' she asked shortly as they went to join the others. 'Basile—that's the boatman—can't. All the others can, but a couple not well, so if anything goes wrong I'm saving you last.'

'I can swim,' he assured her amusedly. 'And I've been diving around the Indian Ocean for years, so you'll be able to give your undivided attention to the paying customers. But what are you expecting to go wrong?'

'Nothing,' she snapped, rattled.

The boat arrived while she was introducing him. Noting the reaction from the three female members of the party to his presence, Lucia shook her head disgustedly. How could he imagine anyone found his pretended attachment to her credible when it was so obvious that he could have just about any woman he chose? These three all had perfectly nice husbands as far as she could tell—one was actually on her honeymoon—but they were looking at Rob as if he had only to beckon and they would follow him to the ends of the earth.

Having him on board put her on her mettle, Lucia soon discovered. She was good with people anyway, and she was kept busy answering the group's questions and pointing out anything she thought might be of interest, such as the barracuda she spotted chasing a shoal of smaller fish when they were out on deep water, and later some big tunny.

They weren't only interested in things marine either. The women, all in their late twenties or early thirties, wanted to know about the various ways of wearing a pareo, and Lucia happily stood up to demonstrate all the methods she had learnt both here and during the periods her father had worked in Mauritius.

She became aware of Rob's leisurely appraisal as she released herself from one of the more intricate arrangements, standing revealed in her plain sea-green one-piece. The other men were enjoying the display too, she noticed, but she didn't mind them. It was just Rob, sitting there and looking at her like that, with a slight smile of enjoyment playing about his mouth, whom she found so disconcerting.

'That's about the lot,' she told the women, quickly retying the pareo in the way she preferred and flashing their husbands a reproving smile. 'Show's over.'

It was because of what had happened last night that she was so acutely aware of Rob now, she supposed, and she guessed that it would be some time before she was able to forget the way he had made her feel. But he needn't have sat there looking at her as if her swimsuit simply didn't exist—and why had he had to take his shirt off?

All the men were shirtless, in fact, but she was hardly aware of the others. Rob, though! Shooting him surreptitious little glances from behind the protection of her dark lenses, Lucia discovered that her throat had gone dry, and she swallowed. He really was something—so magnificently made, and the strong, sexy impression somehow enhanced by his deep tan and dark chest hair.

They were heading south, the island coast still within sight, when they encountered a large school of dolphins, and Lucia spoke to Basile in the Comorean language, a kind of Creole, asking him to slow the craft.

The sea's friendliest, most curious creatures immediately approached to play about the boat, keeping up with it and winning enchanted exclamations from the party. Aware of Rob now standing beside her, Lucia removed her sunglasses and looked down at the dolphins, her face tight with reluctance.

But then, glancing briefly at the group and seeing the rapt expressions, her natural inclination to give pleasure triumphed over her loathing of deep water. Telling Basile to stop the engine properly, she whipped off her pareo, dropped it and her glasses, took a step up and dived neatly over the side of the boat.

The dolphins immediately streaked to welcome her and stayed to play. They encouraged her, and she them, and they dived and surfaced together, racing and chasing, Lucia letting them catch her and bump against her in the gentle way that seemed to signal affectionate acceptance.

Surfacing, she trod water and looked back at her entranced audience.

'Those of you who are good swimmers in deep water are welcome to join me. It's quite safe,' she called, but it seemed that they all preferred to watch, still commenting excitedly, cameras clicking busily, so she let the entertainment continue a while.

Finally, with a glance at the sun to see how much time had passed, she abandoned the sport, patting the round head of the particularly attentive dolphin who had adopted her as his special friend and, seeing he was willing, giving him a quick kiss as a finale, to a burst of delighted laughter from the boat.

Then she let a swell of warm water carry her to the side of the craft and he followed, reluctant to let her go, only giving her a last loving nudge of farewell when she put up a hand to pull herself back on board.

It would have to be Rob who helped her up! As she stood swaying slightly he steadied her, and she was shockingly conscious of his sun-warmed flesh just touching her water-cooled body. Her mind had gone blank, dolphins, her duties and the other people on board all forgotten as she was assaulted by an involuntary tug of strong, sweet sensation deep down inside her.

'You really are a mermaid, aren't you?' Rob murmured, his glance enigmatic as it swept over the wet hair plastered to her skull and her skin, silvered by myriad drops of water now that she stood in the sun.

He still had hold of her by the arms, his fingers light and warm, and her interior reaction to the contact momentarily became as powerful as the sea itself, imitating the pull and surge of its rhythmic responses to the moon and making her expression vulnerable.

Then her face closed as she finally registered what he had said, and she moved stiffly away out of his reach.

'It's nearly always safe to go in when there are dolphins around, because they'd warn me if there was any danger and do their best to help me if anything did go wrong,' she said rather stiltedly, almost as if in excuse, before turning with a rueful smile to include the others in what she had to say.

'They're beautiful creatures, aren't they? But, you know, I've never really been sure of the wisdom of encouraging them to come around us. They're so curious and trusting, it makes them vulnerable. They want to be friends, but should we let them?'

It started a debate and the couples had dozens of questions as the dolphins continued to follow the boat for a while after she'd asked Basile to get it moving again. Lucia was glad, as it prevented her thinking too much about what had happened when Rob had helped her back on board—although she remained acutely conscious of him, especially as he was observing her so thoughtfully, a strange combination of knowledge and curiosity darkening his eyes.

Why couldn't he wear dark glasses like her? Then she wouldn't have to see his expression, and be disconcerted.

After a while the three couples fell silent over cold drinks, contentedly dreaming in the sun, only the honeymoon pair murmuring flirtatious secrets to each other at invervals, and after a word with Basile about where she wanted to dive Lucia sat down, dry now and wrapped in her pareo, sunglasses hiding her troubled eyes.

She stirred resentfully as Rob got up and came to sit beside her.

'Can't you at least put your shirt on?' she muttered furiously, and the smile he gave dazzled with an infintely wicked charm.

'Why, am I distracting you?'

'Yes, damn it!'

He seemed to know so much about her that he had probably already known that too, so there was no point in denying it.

Oh, she knew what was wrong with her. Quite simply, she wanted him. That in itself wasn't so bad. It was the intensity of the wanting that appalled her. She had never, ever desired Thierry to such an extent, and she had loved him! She still did, surely? It had only been Saturday when she had arrived, confidently expecting to marry him, and it was just Monday now.

And how could she desire Rob at all when she disliked him? She must be suffering from some surplus of energy now that she no longer had her degree to work towards.

'Calm down; I'm not going to get into a public fight with you. Don't look at me if it helps,' Rob suggested easily, and changed the subject. 'I notice you speak Comorean to Basile?'

'I'm not really fluent. It's a hybrid language.' Lucia seized at the neutral topic with relief, although she realised it had been she who had introduced the personal note, referring to the absence of his shirt. 'A mixture of Arabic, Swahili and other African languages, with quite a bit of French thrown in. Basile sort of personifies the history of the islands as he's descended from both native islanders and French settlers.'

'They're an interesting people, all of them, and some of their customs are unusual.'

'Yes, have you seen all the half-built houses scattered about the island? That's one of my favourites,' she offered, with a quick smile. 'When a daughter is born her father starts building her a house, but because no one is exactly rich the building only proceeds at intervals—bits added here and there whenever Papa can afford it. But things are better now that hotels like yours are increasing the tourist trade.'

Rob was watching her intently, and she had the impression that he was taking mental notes as she spoke. It made her feel shy—inexplicably so, because she had never really suffered from shyness, her nature being essentially outgoing when she wasn't afflicted by rage, resentment and wounded pride, or whatever was troubling her now.

He continued questioning her about the islands, their people and customs, and she answered knowledgeably, half of her glad to be distracted from what lay ahead. She was telling him about the special orchid that grew only on Grande Comore and nowhere else in the world when Basile caught her attention, asking a silent question by raising the black eyebrows that contrasted so beautifully with his exquisite pale-coffee skin.

Lucia looked back to the black volcanic rock on shore to get her bearings and nodded. The boat began to slow, her answers to Rob's questions grew disjointed and she sighed silently, wishing herself ashore even if it meant scorching her feet on that baking black rock.

Tension held her face stiffly expressionless and she sat very still, trying to concentrate her will, gathering courage. Rob had fallen silent, and after a while she got up.

'We're getting to where we're going to dive,' she submitted a little breathlessly. 'I must see if Basile wants to anchor properly.'

As well as Rob, the French pair and both men from Africa intended diving. Apart from Rob, only one had ever tried it before. She had explained the procedure and safety rules to them earlier, but she went over everything again after slithering into the brief warm-water wetsuit she preferred and donning transparent, state-of-the-art flippers.

'Am I all right, please?' she asked Rob, after checking the others' oxygen herself. 'All right, everyone, this should be one of the most fascinating experiences of your lives, but please remember everything I've told you. Keep me in sight at all times, obey my signals, and if you have any problems let me or Rob know by the sign I've shown you. It's not that deep here, as this is the first dive for most of you, but there's a drop nearby—a sort of underwater cliff—that I want you to keep away from because it's for very experienced divers only.'

'Have you been over it?' the South African asked.

'Yes.' Lucia controlled a shudder of remembered revulsion. 'A number of times.'

'You're fine,' Rob told her as she turned to look at him enquiringly, and she was unwillingly grateful to have him diving with her on her first descent after so long away.

She glanced enviously at the two women who were remaining on board, one so dark, the other correspondingly fair, and smiled.

'Cover up if the sun gets too hot,' she reminded them conscientiously, 'and you know where the drinks are if you're thirsty. Basile will look after you.'

She sat down on the edge of the boat, back to the ocean, face set and eyes remote as she sank deep into herself, searching for the determination that had got her through this so many times before.

Then she became aware of Rob observing her with narrowed eyes, so she smiled insouciantly, adjusted her goggles and let herself fall into the water.

CHAPTER SIX

LUCIA pointed out a moray eel to her companions and then indicated that it was time to begin their ascent out of this miraculous underwater garden so lavishly adorned with brilliant colours and strange shapes.

It was such a richly beautiful world down here, but for her the silent loneliness had always nudged mercilessly at education and reason, probing dangerously into suppressed terrors. Even with companions she felt isolated, cut off from all she knew and loved, and thus desperately insecure.

She longed to be up in the sunlight again, preferably on dry land, and when Rob signalled that she should go up with the others and that he would come last she obeyed, despite her rebelling pride, telling herself firmly that no one would guess at the weakness that made her so grateful for the offer.

Once safely back on board, she made sure that everyone was all right and satisfied and helped them free of their equipment, stowing it neatly away. Then, when she had seen Rob join them, she stripped off her own gear and sat down on one of the boat's low, bench-like seats, almost huddling, with her pareo wrapped right round her as if it were a blanket.

That she had survived once more was the simplest of her thankful reflections as she waited to feel warm again. With the ordeal safely behind her, she was aware, as always, of how irrational her loathing and fear were, and she tried not to think of all the other descents she would have to make with other holiday-makers in the days to come.

The others were happily discussing all that they had

done, felt and seen, and Rob came over to where she sat a little apart from them.

'Are you all right?' he asked her expressionlessly.

'Yes!' She had forgotten to put her sunglasses on again and her blue-green eyes blazed with unguarded relief as she gave him the fervent answer.

'Sure?'

A hard, sceptical note arrested her attention and she was surprised to detect a glint of anger in his eyes. Alerted, she resolutely encased herself in control, needing the armour, and gave him a defiant smile.

'It was a good dive, they're all pleased, so the day is a success. I hope you're now satisfied that I can do the job?'

The anger didn't go away. If anything, it became more pronounced, tightening his face and hardening the mouth which she was learning to view as a guide to what he was feeling.

'Oh, yes, Lucia,' Rob conceded harshly, 'You're very proficient, very professional. Congratulations.'

Then he turned away and left her alone.

She knew that she ought to be satisfied, but his manner perplexed her. Finally she gave a mental shrug. He was probably just annoyed at finding that he had no grounds for depriving her of the job that Chester had given her and subsequently somehow ensuring that she left the Comoros.

He continued to ignore her. The couple from the Ivory Coast had some connection with the tourist industry in their own country, and the conversation they got into with Rob kept the three of them going all through lunch and during the time that Lucia spent taking a couple of the party snorkelling in the shallower waters they had headed for.

When they arrived back at the Ballard Hotel's beach in the late afternoon Rob said a pleasant general farewell to the party, but all Lucia got was a brief inclination of the head and a last angry look. Then he turned and stalked away up the beach.

Well, that suited her perfectly, she decided rebelliously. She didn't want anything more to do with him and it seemed that the feeling was mutual. And yet she couldn't stop herself wondering what was wrong, and whether he had temporarily forgotten the deception they were supposed to be practising.

Reaching her room, Lucia washed her hair under the shower, using a liberal quantity of conditioner, and when it was dry she put on a low-necked black cotton-knit shirt and a pretty pair of shorts with tiny black flowers on a white background, the few pleats gathered into a belted waistband flattering to her slim figure.

She looked at herself in the mirror for a moment, pleased with the slight tan that she had very carefully allowed herself to acquire during the course of the day and the few fair highlights that now glinted in her hair.

Then, having found out from Madelon that staff members were permitted to sign for drinks against their salaries, she took herself along to the open-air bar where she had been yesterday for one. She deserved a drink, she decided.

She had almost finished it when a young woman approached the small table at which she was sitting alone. She was momentarily startled, having almost forgotten Nadine Ballard's existence. Somehow she had been reduced to a cipher in this whole uncomfortable mess.

'Lucia?' she ventured tentatively as Lucia stiffened. 'I'm Nadine Ballard.'

'Yes, I know,' Lucia offered warily.

'May I sit down?' She waited for Lucia's reluctant nod before doing so. 'I wanted to talk to you, because Thierry can't or won't tell me much yet, and I need to know. . .'

'If it's all right?' Lucia supplied flatly as Nadine's voice trailed away, and she wondered tiredly if these constant trials of her strength would ever come to an end.

'Something like that,' Nadine agreed faintly.

Lucia examined her with a certain amount of curiosity, this girl who had stolen Thierry from her. At present she sounded vulnerable, but her still, oval face expressed only a calm resolve, and Lucia gained an impression of inner strength. Secretly, she had to admit that Nadine seemed to be the sort of person she usually admired and sometimes wished she could be—serene and utterly unaggressive.

'Well, it is,' she assured her brightly, managing a careless smile, acting for all she was worth. 'Thierry is the past. I think we became a habit to each other; that's why it lasted so long—why we let it drift into more than it should have been, even to an engagement.'

'He said something similar,' Nadine confessed with evident relief, missing the way that Lucia's eyes flashed.

'I was between school and varsity when I met him— a child, really. I've changed, moved on.' Lucia reflected tartly that she would soon have herself convinced, and she gestured rather coyly. 'But, anyway, I thought you knew that your brother and I have. . .got a thing for each other.'

If Rob was still intent on keeping up the pretence!

'Yes, but I'm assuming that it's as temporary as all his other affairs—and assuming that you know that too,' Nadine added anxiously. 'He's usually fair that way—warning the girls.'

'Of course,' Lucia agreed blithely.

'I was concerned that you might think you could have Thierry back when it was over.' An implacable note made it clear that Nadine wouldn't countenance any such thing, and Lucia shook her head cheerfully, earning a gratified smile, and now it was Nadine's turn to regard her curiously.

'I was surprised about you and Rob, I have to say, when it's obvious that you must be dedicated to your future career—what with having got a degree in marine biology and all. It's not that he's sexist or anything like that, but he has always avoided any sort of personal involvement with women like you ever since Shelagh reinforced the prejudices our mother created in him.'

'Shelagh?'

'The only woman he ever considered having a permanent relationship with—but it turned out to be disastrous, so it's fortunate they never got as far as marriage. She was a Zimbabwean, like us, but she was always away up in Kenya or Rwanda or somewhere, spending months on end studying some kind of anthropoids.'

'Oh, I think he did mention her, but not her name,' Lucia realised, recalling his reference to an ex-girl-friend working with primates.

So maybe, if he was prejudiced against career women, today's proof of her absolute professionalism with regard to her new job had been responsible for the hostility that Rob had shown her since they had dived.

Obviously he had never got over this Shelagh woman. He had said he liked warm, generous, emotional women, who gave all of themselves to a relationship, so he must be capable of the same, and yet, as Nadine had just confirmed, all his relationships were temporary, so he must still be in love with Shelagh.

Lucia picked up her glass and drained it as Nadine said earnestly, 'I will make Thierry happy, Lucia.'

'And he you?' Lucia made it a question.

'Oh, yes!' Nadine was confident. 'I've had some horrible experiences—it's to do with my being so quiet—but I knew as soon as I met Thierry. All relationships make demands—difficult ones—but one thing I know he'll never do is hit me.'

'No, he'll never do that,' Lucia confirmed quietly, sure in her knowledge of Thierry as she pushed back her chair, suddenly glad for Nadine if she had the horror of violence in her past. 'I do wish you both all the happiness in the world, Nadine. Will you excuse me, please? I think Chester Watson is looking for me.'

It wasn't an excuse. Chester was hovering a short distance away and Lucia went to see what he wanted with an odd feeling of relief. Nadine would make Thierry happy—but why should the knowledge please her? She loved him herself, didn't she? She wanted to be the one to make him happy, the one who shared his home and settled family tradition.

'I can't find Rob to tell him, but I've thought it over, and that yachtsman I told you about is still available to do the boat trips,' Chester announced mysteriously as she reached him and they moved out of hearing range of the evening drinkers.

'Madelon Brouard is taking over Nadine's job, so what I've decided is that you should go into the hotel shop, Lucia—you told me you you have till experience—as well as doing her share of the minibus tours she escorted round the island on certain days. Rob says you're incredibly knowledgeable on all sorts of fascinating aspects, whereas Madelon had to swot it up.'

Lucia's immediate reaction was one of absolute joy, but then other things began to sink in.

'What has Rob got to do with this?' she asked suspiciously. 'He found me competent! He said I was proficient and professional. . . He has *told* you to take me off the boat trips, hasn't he?'

Chester looked dismayed. 'Oh, now, love, I had no idea I'd be causing trouble between the two of you! How was I to know he's the old-fashioned sort who doesn't discuss things with the little woman? He doesn't come across like that. I thought it was a joint decision, that you'd talked about it since you've got something going between you.'

'He never said a word!' Raging resentment was gathering in Lucia's breast. 'He said I was good! So why has he done this?'

Chester threw out his hands. 'How should I know? Maybe he's being protective if he doesn't like the idea of his woman taking risks—because, let's face it, there is an element of danger to most activities that involve the sea.'

'I'm going to find him and ask him,' Lucia declared contemptuously.

'Well, just remember—and you can tell him too—I'm not responsible if you have a row and break up over this.'

Whether Chester had tried Rob's suite or not, that was where Lucia found him. He opened the door immediately in response to her furiously thumping fist.

'Not another rage,' he remarked with amused exasperation as he saw her face.

'Why have you told Chester to take me off the boat trips?' she demanded stormily, and heard him swear succinctly. 'You said you didn't interfere, and now you've done this! It's to drive me off the island, isn't it? Having to pretend you're involved with me is too much of a nuisance; it's stopping you going after Madelon! Well, tough; your precious sister is just going to have to put up with seeing me around, because Chester has offered me a job in the shop and escorting bus tours, and I'm going to take it.'

'I suggested that he should offer you something of the sort,' Rob snapped, closing the door now that she had marched into the suite.

'But why?' she responded passionately. 'You said I was *good*!'

It was a wounded pride's cry of protest, and he was silent, eyes unfathomable as he studied her stricken expression, although there was a distinct tightness about his mouth.

'You're brilliant,' he affirmed eventually, and swore again. 'I should have ensured that Chester didn't involve me when he told you. That's why I didn't discuss it with you.'

'Why?' Her voice had gone shaky.

'You're not going to like it,' he warned her tautly. 'I didn't think you needed the humiliation.'

'Proficient and professional, you said,' she reminded him.

'And terrified, Lucia,' Rob asserted softly.

She stared at him in utter disbelief for a moment before dropping her eyes, her face flaming. How had he known? No one else had ever guessed, not even her father once he had forgotten that first childish display of fear.

'How did you know?' she asked in an agonised whisper, quite incapable of assembling any sort of defence. 'How can you know me like that?'

Rob was silent for a moment, his expression as complicated as if he was entertaining some thought he didn't much care for. Then he shrugged.

'I just seem to know you,' he allowed dismissively. 'You are frightened of the sea, aren't you, Lucia? You were so incredibly tense before you dived, so relieved after you were up. You weren't even that enthusiastic about going in with the dolphins earlier, although you did so voluntarily in the end. But it was the others' delight, plus the safety factory inherent in the dolphins' presence, that finally decided you.'

'All right!' Lucia had hold of herself now, but her voice was raw and choking with resentment as she admitted, 'I'm a coward! I'm not physically adventurous! I hate deep water and I am not the mermaid everyone around here keeps calling me!'

'In a literal sense I think we may both be glad of that,' Rob observed, with a disconcerting gleam of humour in his eyes. But even more disconcerting was the gentleness of tone with which he continued, 'And you are not a coward, Lucia, you're the reverse. You did it, you went down, and your first care was always for the others with you. None of them guessed the truth.'

Lucia stared at him wonderingly, something hard and hurting in her breast easing slightly in response to his words.

'That's why you sent me up before you, isn't it?' she realised, humiliation returning, and with it the habitual need to hide it by attacking. 'I suppose you're going to come over all manly and encouraging, and make it your business to convince me there's nothing to be afraid of, and help me overcome my fear. Don't! I am afraid and I always will be.'

'Of course you are, so give in to it. Never go into the water again if you don't want to. We're all obliged to do some things we don't want to, from the day we're first sent to school, and simply living and interacting with other human beings uses up most of the courage we're given, so why should any of us force ourselves when it's something that's not essential?

'When we're forcing ourselves physically it means someone or something is imposing on us and our individual right to have preferences. You're an adult. If you don't like doing something and don't want to, then don't do it—don't force yourself. Stay out of the sea; stand in the sun, Lucia, if that's what you want to do.'

He had defeated her anger and she gave him another wondering look, knowing an urge to surrender to the understanding that he was offering.

'I'd like that,' she confided slowly.

'Why have you forced yourself in the past, though?' Rob asked.

'My dad. . .' She hesitated, groping for the answer she had never before had to put into actual words.

'Your father forced you to dive?' A spark of cold anger had appeared in his eyes, banishing the smoky mystery and leaving them hard and brilliant.

'No!' Sensitive to the censure, Lucia was indignant. 'He just. . . It was—Look, when I was very little I was scared of the water, and I saw how disappointed he was, so I made myself. . . It's no big deal! I just did it because I knew he wanted me to be able to. I didn't have to like it, and after a while I got so good at it all— swimming and the rest—that he forgot I'd ever been afraid.'

'So you forced yourself, to please him?' Rob probed, still sounding sharply critical.

'I said it's not big deal!' she snapped.

'All right, it's no big deal!' The repitition came with an air of mockery, as if he was humouring her, and she glared at him distrustfully.

'So I don't want you feeling sorry for me, as if I'm one of those people who've been damaged in their childhood,' she instructed him, with a jerky little lift of her chin. 'I wanted to please him. And there's another thing—this new job you say you recommended I should have? You've said the Ballard Group isn't a charity, and I won't have—'

'I'm very close to losing my temper with you, you impossible girl,' Rob interrupted. 'Why don't you sit down and *calm* down? I've seen for myself today that you are good with people, interested and interesting, so you'd get on well in most jobs which involve dealing with them.

'It's a natural ability that's going to go to waste once you can afford to leave here and find the sort of post for which you're qualified. I imagine you'll choose to spend most of your life working in laboratories as you're such a contradiction—a trained marine biologist who fears the water.'

'I may decide to do something else entirely,' Lucia submitted vaguely, turning and accepting the invitation to sit down just so that her expression might be hidden from him for a few seconds.

But her studiedly casual tone must have given her away, because when she looked up from her new position on the couch Rob's eyes were glittering with realisation.

'Just a moment!' he rapped, but then his voice went very soft as he asked, 'How much else have you done to please your father? How many other natural inclinations have you denied? Didn't you *want* to be a marine biologist?'

Frustratedly she thumped a fist down on the arm of the couch.

'I hate the way you know everything! Yes, all right, I didn't. And I know I'm cheating him in a sense, because I'd rather not ever use my degree, but I've given three years of my life to keep my promise and I don't think I can give any more. I've got to live my own life—find somewhere to belong and do the things I want to do!'

It was a guiltily defiant protest. 'I think now that my mother tried to make me see that I needn't even go for the degree, that he couldn't be hurt once he was dead—but I didn't listen.'

'No, somehow I don't quite see you as the sort of girl who listens much to her mother,' Rob inserted sardonically.

'And I'd made an actual promise, in so many words, when he had the heart attack and we knew he was dying. It was important enough for him to think of in his last moments, when he told us there was enough money. . .' Lucia's voice faded and she shook her head slightly, trying to rid herself of the weight of the unhappy anger that came with looking back. 'So I did it. Maybe I cheated someone else too—out of the place I had at varsity. I don't know. I've often felt guilty about using the money for something I didn't want, when someone like Hassan Mohammed would have loved the same opportunity in a different faculty but his family couldn't afford it for him.

'I'm glad your hotel is here for him now and he has such good prospects, because he's ambitious... Oh, I know I'm a cheat in all sorts of ways!'

'Hassan is important to you, isn't he?'

The question was distracting, but she nodded. 'We moved around so much that it was difficult to keep the friends I made in various places, but he really made an effort to stay in touch.'

'It seems to me it's yourself you've cheated first and foremost,' Rob remarked tautly, after spending a second or two digesting her answer. 'Or are you going to tell me that this was no big deal either?'

'I wanted to do it. I loved my dad!' She was rebelliously challenging. 'Is there something wrong with that?'

'Not a thing, but there's a whole lot wrong with making sacrifices for love. Three years of your life— and Thierry Olivier too, Lucia?' he prompted.

She shrugged indifferently, pride to the fore. 'I can live with it.'

'You'll have to. So all that, for love.' There was a sharp edge of disgust to the reflection, and she could see the glint of anger in his eyes as he stood in front of her.

'What are you so cross about? Is it because it seems you actually got something wrong, and that now you think I'm not that abomination, the single-minded career woman, you might have to like me a little better?' Lucia taunted.

'Don't let it concern you. I was trying to find a way of breaking it to my dad that I'd really like to go to the South African hotel school or maybe try some kind of personnel work when he had the heart attack. Maybe I'll finally get the chance to pursue something of the sort now that I'm not going to be marrying Thierry.'

'Which tells me just what kind of sacrifices you were prepared to make for *him*, so maybe you really did love him after all,' Rob conceded disparagingly. 'I don't think I want to hear about any others there would have been.'

'Not sacrifices! You seem to have some weirdly limited ideas about what loving someone really means,' she lashed at him. 'It's wanting to make them happy!'

'At whatever cost to yourself?' he derided. 'Maybe your father and Olivier should have given an occasional thought to your happiness.'

'My dad didn't know I wanted to do other things.' She quickly defended her father.

'And Olivier?' His remark was perceptive, in response to the omission.

'It's rather obvious that Thierry didn't love me properly, isn't it?' she reminded him bitterly. 'He needed me to be at home and I'd have been glad to do it because it would have been my home too, even if. . . Only that's all over now, of course. He has got Nadine.'

'He'd never have made you happy,' Rob asserted bitingly.

'Or me him?' she prompted, then took a deep breath and added, 'Nadine will, though. Make him happy.'

'It's not really his welfare that bothers me.'

A slight frown was pulling his dark eyebrows together, so she said quietly, 'He'll never physically abuse her, Rob.'

'How do you know about that?'

'I saw her earlier, before I came up here,' she explained. 'She came looking for me.'

'What for?' he demanded suspiciously.

'To find out if it was all right for her to steal Thierry from me,' she volunteered flippantly.

'What did you tell her?'

'To go right ahead and good luck. . .that sort of civilised thing,' Lucia offered tartly as she stood up.

'You'd better have meant it,' Rob warned her harshly before asking, 'Did she actually tell you about the violence she has endured in her past relationships?'

'I realised when she said she knew Thierry would never hit her.' Meeting his questioning look, she added soberly, 'He never will, Rob. I know that for a fact. I know him.'

'And you loved him,' he supplemented on a note of acceptance, and the horrified thought that he might be starting to pity her slammed into her consciousness.

'Relax! You don't have to have your loyalties divided by needing to feel sorry for me!' She gave him a brightly insouciant smile. 'I'm not hurt by what Thierry has done. I don't care!'

'Pride or truth, Lucia?' Rob urged, gently mocking, and in the briefest of pauses that followed Lucia gained the impression that he was about to say one thing but changed his mind. Instead he came out with, 'But either way I'm delighted to hear it, as long as you don't change your mind and decide you want him back after all.

'Unfortunately you're not going to be able to demonstrate how little you care by parading your new interest tonight—I've accepted an invitation to dinner at the Olivier place and I don't imagine you've got any wild craving to spend an evening there, although it would be perfectly appropriate for me to arrive with the latest woman in my life.'

'Beth Olivier made it abundantly clear that I'm not welcome there,' Lucia reminded him tightly.

'I'll make some excuse for you if Nadine wonders why I'm not running true to form.'

'Why don't you just tell her we've discovered we're incompatible?' she returned shortly, moving towards the door. 'Then you could take Madelon with you.'

'Are we so incompatible? There's at least one area in which we're wholly compatible, I think.' Rob was blocking her way, giving her a lazily challenging smile. 'What happened when I helped you back onto the boat after you'd been in with the dolphins today, Lucia?'

Forced to halt, unless she wanted to collide with him, Lucia regarded him warily. She didn't suppose that there was any point in denying what had happened when he was so infuriatingly knowledgeable about her.

'I believe it's called lust,' she allowed sweetly. 'Excuse me, please. I must go.'

'I believe it's called sexual attraction.' Seeing resentment blaze in her eyes, he added gently, 'It happened to me too, you know.'

'So? That doesn't mean we have to do anything about it.'

She had no intention of exploring any physical attraction, mutual or not, with a man who didn't respect her—and how could he when he was prepared to blackmail her? He probably despised her, in fact, for submitting to it, however practical her reasons.

At the same time she was conscious of a powerfully yearning sensation deep within her as she let her eyes sweep over him, trying to pinpoint exactly what it was about him that drew her so strongly,

His dark face was unusual, not conventionally handsome at all but undeniably and devastatingly attractive, and the mystery of his mouth, which could be so many things, was shockingly arresting; it took an effort of will to drag her gaze away from its evocative curve and complete the inspection. The trousers and casual shirt he had on were subtly suited to his lean strength and vibrant potency, and Lucia was again subject to the inner lurching sensation which she recognised as signalling the onset of erotic hunger.

'Of course we don't,' Rob was agreeing smoothly as he lifted a hand to her shoulder.

He let it rest there a few seconds before encircling her shoulders with his arm, pulling her close. Then, instead of kissing her as she was half anticipating, he simply stood there holding her like that with one arm, the other relaxed at his side.

After a moment Lucia lowered her head, and she was aware of his bent over it. She had a sense of something oddly intent in his attitude, as if he was listening, or noting and absorbing whatever messages she was conveying to him with her stillness.

'Is this—that relaxation thing again?' she mumbled dislocatedly.

'If you like. Whatever you want it to be.' Rob sounded idly indulgent.

But sharpened consciousness of him as a man precluded relaxation now. Obedient to all manner of inner stirrings, Lucia slipped her arms round him and tipped back her head.

'No,' she said, in a voice slowed and laden with a burden of sensual awareness, not really sure of what she was asking or telling him. His body felt so strong and warm within her slim, embracing arms, and she wanted both desperately—his certain strength and his vital warmth—her need unexpectedly emotional instead of merely physical.

Rob chose to accept that single word as either permission or invitation. Lucia saw his eyes darken just before her own closed, and then he was kissing her. As his tongue nudged gently at hers in assured expectation of her response the internal stirring assailing her intensified to a deep, throbbing disturbance. She had never known a mouth so erotic, waking hers to miraculous, almost unbearably sensitive life.

A hand massaging the low hollow of her back seemed to melt her loins. She felt as if she was composed of liquid heat, a molten, dragging deliquescence down there where softness and gently receptive shaping made her a woman.

She was responding to Rob's kiss with an aching passion, and yet at the same time she felt profoundly vulnerable, as if she was surrendering something essential to herself. Desire was an intolerable weight, oppressing her, depriving her of autonomy, her body's call to his maleness become a heavy, pounding summons.

Control didn't exist, nor did thought, and she complied instinctively when he moved to the couch, pulling her down with him. But then a hand stroking along the taut, silky length of her inner thigh beneath the cuff of her shorts made her stiffen.

The caress was too personal when only one other man had been permitted such intimacies. She wasn't ready for a new man yet. Maybe she never would be. She didn't think she wanted to give another man the chance to reject her as Thierry had done.

And this particular man could only be playing with her, when there were women available to him such as Madelon and all those others she had seen looking at him so hungrily—women far more beautiful, poised and accomplished than she was.

'No?' he queried lightly in response to her resistance, and let her up, following easily after a moment.

Humiliation was scalding. How could she have wanted him when he must either despise or pity her?

'Right again, Rob,' she acknowledged bitterly. 'Just as you've been right about nearly everything to do with me. How do you do it? It's quite a knack.'

His expression defied interpretation as he surveyed

her flushed face, feverishly shining eyes and slightly swollen lips.

'And you hate it, don't you? But you are transparent, Lucia, at least to me. Only, I haven't been right about everything, you know, considering all that I've learned this evening,' he added with unexpected gentleness.

'But you guessed everything before I told you,' she muttered resentfully, not yet in full control of herself, some strengthening purity missing from the anger that she was trying to gather about herself like a protective cloak. 'All right, I know I'm being ungrateful when you've been. . .kind, and I'm sorry.'

She couldn't be sure, but she thought a slight sigh came from Rob just before he smiled. 'I don't believe I'm hearing this!'

'Make the most of it,' she quipped, glad of the lighter moment, but he chose not to prolong it.

'And the things I've learned, I wish I hadn't,' he told her enigmatically. 'You're too emotionally messed up—and you've been messed *around*. Even the most casual sort of involvement with you would be like accompanying you barefoot on a walk across a mile of broken glass, and I'm not a masochist, or into watching others bleed. If you want anything from me, you'll have to sort yourself out.'

She had been right, then. He did pity her. Lucia's chin rose.

'I don't want anything from you, thanks, Rob. I'm off,' she added as it occurred to her that she hadn't actually told Chester Watson that she would take the alternative job he had offered her.

Then a different thought struck her and she hesitated, searching Rob's face reluctantly.

'What?' he asked.

Still she hesitated, finding pride split down the middle by two opposing needs. Finally she gave a defeated little shrug. He knew everything, he knew the worst of her, so why not ask?

'I don't want anyone else knowing—all that you know. About anything.' The jerkily ungracious request sounded more like a demand or even an ill-natured instruction, and, hearing herself, Lucia coloured, lowering her eyes in time to see one of his dark, able hands clench into a fist.

A moment later, however, he had uncurled his fingers and was touching her lightly on the arm in reassurance.

'It's our secret, Lucia,' he promised her.

CHAPTER SEVEN

LUCIA had the elegant hotel shop to herself when Nadine Ballard walked in the following afternoon.

She had spent the day not happily but contentedly, enjoying the contact with the hotel guests who came into the shop, which sold a wide variety of souvenirs, maps and literature about the islands in addition to beachwear and tanning oils and lotions.

Relief at the knowledge that she need not enter deep water again had eased some of her tension, and her mood had been further soothed by the knowledge that she would not have to deal with Rob's disconcerting presence all day. He had sent her a note that morning, telling her that he was flying to one of the archipelago's other islands on business but would be back by the evening, flying conditions permitting.

Pausing in the act of arranging some tubes of cream, in order of their protection factor, alongside a display of sunglasses and hats with a vivid pareo fanned out to form a backdrop, Lucia gave Nadine a quick, contained smile, careful not to offer or invite too much. She had quite liked her, and it had been reassuring to realise that she would make Thierry happy, but she didn't think she wanted to get too friendly.

'Oh, you've changed everything around,' Nadine realised. 'It looks so attractive now.'

'Thank you,' Lucia murmured, and, seeing that Nadine's oval face had grown grave again immediately she'd stopped speaking, she added, 'How can I help you?'

'Lucia, you told me that it was all right. . .about me and Thierry?' Nadine ventured unhappily.

Lucia's face closed defensively. Not again! How much reassurance did she want? But perhaps she had found out that Lucia still had Thierry's ring.

'Of course it is,' she confirmed, blithely dismissive, suppressing an impulse to ask if she would like a certificate of transferred ownership.

'Then why did my brother say such horrible things to Thierry about the way he has treated you when he came to dinner last night?' Nadine demanded, and misinterpreted Lucia's shocked gasp of outrage. 'Oh, he didn't go for him in front of Beth and me, but poor Thierry was so upset that I got it out of him after Rob had left.'

Lucia concentrated on moving a hat in order to conceal the rage that she was sure must be blazing in her eyes.

'Sorry, I know nothing about it.' When she was sure that she had her facial expression under control, she faced Nadine with a shrug. 'It wasn't at my instigation and I don't know why Rob did it. Don't let him spoil things for you and Thierry, Nadine, because I do know that's the last thing he'd want to do.'

Considering the lengths to which he was prepared to go to prevent anything coming between the pair, she reflected acidly.

'Yes, until last night I'd thought he was pleased about our engagement,' Nadine admitted.

'He is, because he knows you'll be safe and happy with Thierry and that's what he wants for you,' Lucia pointed out gently. 'And I know Thierry will be the same with you. I don't know you well enough to be so concerned about your welfare, but if you've had a bad time with other men then I'm glad you've found Thierry.'

'You really do mean it.' The troubled look was beginning to clear from Nadine's eyes. 'I told Rob how nice you'd been when he first arrived last night, because he seemed to think I shouldn't have come to see you, and he was convinced we must have quarrelled.'

Naturally he wouldn't have taken *her* word for it that they hadn't! Lucia managed to keep a smile pinned to her face.

To her relief Nadine didn't stay long, so she wasn't called on to sustain the act for long. Her hypersensitive pride was in revolt over what Rob had taken it on himself to do, and, had he been on the island, fury would have driven her in search of him once more.

His absence frustrated her now and the anger remained with her, although she was forced to push it to the back of her mind by the need to concentrate on other things—making herself agreeable to her customers and being sociable when she ate dinner with some of the hotel staff that night.

She and Hassan Mohammed sat on a while after the meal was over, happily reviving their shared childhood memories and discussing the improvements there had been to the islanders' circumstances since those days.

Taking her leave of him a little later, Lucia hesitated. Rob had sent her that note this morning in case she'd wondered where he was, but she didn't feel inclined to return the courtesy—although she still had every intention of telling him what she thought of him. Additionally there was that act of theirs to be considered, if he still thought it was necessary.

Finally she said casually, 'I think I'm going to spend a while out on the beach, Hassan. If Rob Ballard gets back and you see him, you can tell him that's where I'll be.'

'Sure.' Hassan gave her a quick smile. 'He's great, the way he motivates us all. It was a relief to me to see you with him, you know. When I first heard about Thierry Olivier and Mademoiselle Ballard, I was worried.'

Lucia shrugged, feeling guilty about deceiving a

friend. 'People move on; they find out that the things they thought they wanted no longer seem so important.'

'Like me, having to accept that I couldn't study medicine—' he laughed '—and finding that my heart is in the tourist industry, in which I intend to go even as far as the ministry some day.'

Lucia had the beach to herself at this hour, and she sat cross-legged on the soft ivory sand, facing the ocean beyond which lay Africa. A tropical night breeze came and went capriciously, returning to play lightly over her skin at intervals, too warm and idly tender for her to feel chilled. There was half a moon and the stars were decorative crystal baubles, palely glittering and remote in the inky sky, the occasional streak of a firefly's flight so much warmer and nearer by contrast.

Her mind kept drifting back to Nadine's visit, and it was initially perplexing to discover that she truly was happy for her and Thierry because she knew they would be happy together. In the end, though, she decided it didn't require analysis because the explanation was easy: of course she wanted Thierry to be happy.

The difficult part was acknowledging that he would probably be a lot happier with Nadine than he would have been with her.

But what about her own happiness? Lucia wasn't sure how she felt. Her heart ought to be aching, but it seemed to be in her pride that she was experiencing the most rawly painful wound of all.

She was rejected, discarded, abandoned—and yet, in thinking of what she had lost, she tended to do so more in terms of the emotional security that would have come with a sense of belonging, rather than her actual relationship with Thierry. Too, there were those odd moments when she caught herself looking at her situation with perverse relish, as if it represented—

The long ebony shadow that fell across the pale sand beside her brought a surge of relief, because she had been prey to the uncomfortable conviction that whatever she was groping towards—some piece of self-knowledge—would prove unpalatable at best, and possibly utterly shaming.

'Hassan Mohammed gave me your message,' Rob announced.

'It wasn't a message,' she snapped. 'I merely told him he could tell you where I'd be if he saw you.'

'Ah, yes, of course—to lend colour to our little pretence.'

'It's such a silly business.' Lucia was scornful. 'I don't like deceiving people.'

'Yes, you do,' he contradicted her. 'In this instance, anyway. I don't believe you're habitually dishonest.'

'No, only when I'm forced to be,' she retorted resentfully.

'Oh, I know you've kept referring to blackmail, but you've played along so consistently and nicely that it must be necessary to you,' Rob guessed, softly derisive, and she supposed it was, but she wasn't going to admit as much out loud. 'But perhaps the charade is frustrating you where Hassan is concerned?'

'Why have you got this idea about him and me?' Curiosity distracted her.

'He's obviously acquainted with a softer, warmer side of you. Then again, I can see that side for myself when you mention him. He's one person who doesn't seem to arouse your hostility,' Rob observed challengingly.

'Because he's one person who has never harmed me in any way,' she snapped. 'That makes him my friend, and that's what he's going to stay. We go back too far to hold any mystery for each other—which I would have said was a prerequisite for romance.'

He laughed softly. 'I don't think there are any hard and fast rules.'

Lucia had to laugh too. 'In fact, I told him something similar earlier. He's one of those ambitious people who has got his whole future plotted out. When his career reaches an appropriate stage he intends to find someone suitable to marry, but, being an idealist as well, he's also *planning* to fall in love with her. I told him it doesn't work like that, and that it will serve him right if he falls in love with someone totally unsuitable.'

'It happens,' Rob agreed rather drily, and Lucia knew that he must be thinking about Shelagh, whose devotion to her career had made her so unsuitable for him but whom he must still love, as he had failed to settle down with any other, more suitable woman.

'I did want to see you, though.' She changed the subject, what he had done returning to the front of her mind.

'No, don't get up,' he adjured, seeing her intention and dropping gracefully into a relaxed position beside her on the sand.

He was too close and Lucia tensed, uncertain, but a vision of herself standing up and railing at him while he reclined at her feet was too ridiculous to be contemplated, and the thought pulled her lips into a reluctant little smile for a moment.

Then anger forced its way back.

'What do you think you were doing, attacking Thierry last night? Nadine told me,' she offered accusingly. 'I asked you, and you promised not to let anyone else know the things—that you know about me. That was an abuse of my trust. All right, I should have known better than to put my faith in you, when you don't owe me anything and you haven't shown me any sort of regard or even consideration before. But it was also an abuse of—of your gift! That horrible way you've got of. . .of knowing me. Telling him what he'd done to me like that. I have got some pride, you know.'

The trite conclusion prompted a snatch of sardonic laughter that made her skin prickle.

'That's an understatement if ever I heard one. No, be quiet, you difficult girl,' he added peremptorily as she drew a sharp breath. 'You really are the touchiest, most impossible person I know, forever attacking me over this, that and the other, and always without possessing all the facts. I know you? It's time you got to know me, Lucia—to know that you can and should trust me.

'I will never do anything to add to the humiliation you've endured over this business—and I do know how much you hate my knowing, but neither of us could have helped that, given the circumstances, and I won't pretend I *don't* know. You're almost inclined to blame me for the whole thing, aren't you? Still hating me for being the messenger. . .

'Whatever Nadine said, she can't have known the facts either. I don't suppose Olivier went into detail about what I said. I remembered you'd told me you'd let him believe our fiction for some reason—whether out of pride, to ease his conscience or to make him jealous in the hope of winning him back—so I made it very clear to him that his engagement to Nadine had come as an absolute relief to you, that you'd realised you were too special for him and were relishing your freedom. All right?'

The last bit came too close to something she had been fumbling for earlier, and she was silent for several seconds. Finally she nodded, before realising that perhaps he couldn't see her.

'Yes,' she allowed curtly, and then, because she wasn't ready to give up the fight quite yet, asked stiffly, 'But why did you have to say anything to him about it at all?'

'The guy irritated me,' Rob volunteered flatly, 'sitting there basking in the approval of Nadine and his mother, all untroubled because everyone—including you, apparently—has let him get away far too easily with what is unacceptable behaviour by any standards, although I can guess why he did it that way. I am human—I gave in to my irritation and let him know that not everyone views him so indulgently.'

'Then you were. . .cruel,' Lucia ventured slowly. 'He's so sensitive—'

'Stop trying to defend him,' Rob cut in edgily. 'He doesn't deserve it. If you want to know, in attempting to justify himself he had a go at turning the whole thing round and blaming you.'

'I can imagine,' she affirmed sadly.

'He was highly uncomplimentary about you and how inadequate you've been—absent all the time—and would still have been, had he married you,' Rob swept on mercilessly. 'For instance, I gather you were distinctly reluctant to provide him with a family.'

At last—at long last—the moment came when she could direct her rage squarely and solely at Thierry.

'Why should I have wanted children with him?' she retaliated savagely. 'I was going to have to be a mother anyway, to him—'

'Oh, Lucia, that's a terrible betrayal,' Rob mocked bitingly as she broke off, stricken as she realised the same thing.

She wasn't sure if it was a betrayal of Thierry or herself, and she didn't think she cared about the former, because she owed him no loyalty now, especially when he himself had already talked about her so treacherously to this man.

She shrugged defensively. 'Except that I had almost made up my mind to agree to start a family at once, as he wanted, to make up for his having to wait all these years. I also thought it might bring out a. . .sort of stronger, supportive side of his nature that seems to have disappeared since I first met him, because children are vulnerable. Anyway, I do...I did want children eventually. I like them, although I'm not sure what sort of mother I would have made.'

'Will make. I can't see you letting one broken engagement drive you to a nunnery, and you will get over Olivier, Lucia. You'll be a good mother,' Rob added surprisingly, and the sincerity she heard there created an area of warmth around her heart.

'But Olivier would have gone on leaning on you just because you are strong, and even when you're not you pretend well enough to be convincing. You're right, you'd have needed to be a mother to him too, whereas Nadine brings out that strength you mentioned because she is less obviously strong herself.

'You'd have ended up martyring yourself, or else out of control, tripping on power. You must have accepted that by now? He and my sister suit each other. You can't imagine you're still in—'

'I don't want to talk about it yet,' Lucia interrupted hurriedly, with a strangely desperate feeling.

'Or think about it? All right,' he allowed quietly, and when he spoke again it was to ask lightly, 'What were you doing out here? Communing with nature?'

'I'm not that fond of nature,' she confided, feeling almost shy now she had nothing to fight about or against.

'I guessed.'

'People,' she added self-consciously. 'They're what I like.'

'People—so why were you all alone, as you've implied that you weren't actually waiting for me?'

A nervous little laugh escaped her as she realised that she was about to take a major leap forward by admitting, 'I wanted to sit and look at the sea and think about how I don't have to dive any more, only then I didn't. . . Other things got in the way.'

Other freedoms. A treacherous thought.

'They do that.'

'I'm glad I don't have to dive. I'm glad you. . .knew, and told Chester to take me off the trips. I. . .I thank you,' she concluded with stilted formality; admitting to any weakness was so new and difficult for her that she couldn't be entirely natural about it.

'It's all right, Lucia,' he said, his unemphatic tone and absence of mockery making it easier for her to relax. 'None of us likes having other people knowing our vulnerabilities, but you do need someone to know for you. I think we all do—or we become our own oppressors if we never share them, whether through inhibition, pride or whatever.'

'I know. . .I often have too much pride,' she confessed awkwardly, venturing further into this new territory of sharing. 'It has been a problem.'

'But you've needed it just lately.'

He still spoke with the easy, neutral tone of comprehension, still without derision, so this baring of some of her secrets wasn't quite as hard as she might have imagined, especially when he was someone who seemed to know most of them in advance anyway.

It occurred to her that he was being kind because he pitied her, but even that only troubled her a little for the moment. She was more inclined to think how nice he was. She liked him.

The discovery surprised her, but it gave her something else to tell him while she was in this honest mood.

'Rob?'

'Yes?'

'I don't hate you for being the messenger any more.' It still didn't come entirely easily, but it was softly sincere.

There was a brief silence which wasn't truly a silence.

Lucia listened to soft sounds—the sough of the palms behind them and the heaving sighs of the sea's suck and swell before them.

Then Rob said, 'You've come a long way in a very short space of time, haven't you? Three and a half days?'

'Further than anyone can know,' she agreed in a small, fine voice, following her words with a faint breath of laughter. 'Anyone except you, of course.'

'Yes.'

He stirred. Lucia was still sitting cross-legged, comfortable in wash-softened denim shorts and a white blouse, sleeveless and collarless. Now she felt his hand come to rest on the bare curve of the knee nearest to him, and she could accept its warm weight without tensing in this strange mood of surrender that had fallen over her.

She thought it must be simply because she was tired, taxed beyond her strength and resistance by the emotional demands she had faced and met since Saturday afternoon—the need to fight, to be angry, to pretend.

Now there was nothing left, at least temporarily. She thought about asking him about his business on the other island that he had visited today, and then it occurred to her that she ought to remove his hand from her knee before the warm sensation of weakness pervading her became irresistible.

'Are you going to put another hotel in the Comoros?' she wondered, her voice languid as she put out a hand to grasp his wrist.

'It's a real possibility after the discussions I had today,' Rob confirmed, and then there was a pause before he asked, 'Lucia, what are you doing?'

Yes, what? Lucia was appalled, her face heating. Her fingers seemed to have a will of their own. Instead of lifting his hand from her knee, they were travelling slowly up over the underside of his forearm, circling his elbow and straying inquisitively beneath the sleeve of the casual shirt that he was wearing with a pair of jeans. Acutely embarrassed, she snatched her hand away.

'Nothing—I'm sorry...I don't know. Do you live in one of your hotels?' she asked agitatedly, realising that she didn't know where his home was or even if he had one.

'I have suites kept for my exclusive use in all of them, as I travel a lot. There's a house in Zimbabwe—Harare—for when I want to get right away from the business. I'm still a citizen there.'

As he spoke he slid his hand from her knee, his palm flattening as he stroked it over her inner thigh, and this time Lucia let him complete the caress. She knew she shouldn't. She ought to be putting space between them. But she couldn't make herself do the things her mind was dictating. Instead she leaned closer, letting her head rest against his shoulder.

Her hand moved to cover his where it lay on her thigh, his long fingers still stirring slightly in idle play, making her skin tingle deliciously. Hers didn't stay still either, tracing the shape of his hand, finding it beautiful in its capable masculine strength.

Then Rob moved, freeing his hand and lifting it, altering his position so that he could curl his arm right round her shoulders, letting her lean in to him more fully, taking most of her slight weight.

A small, unevenly darting line of light marked the passage of an errant firefly, and Lucia followed its flight with her eyes, breathing in the scents of island vanilla, the sea's salt and Rob's special male fragrance.

She liked the feeling of closeness between them. At one level she was embarrassed by how much she had revealed to him during their short acquaintance, and especially tonight, but in conflict with pride's peculiar sensitivities was releif that someone should know her so well, obviating any need to pretend because to do so would have been pointless. It meant that she could relax for once, and soak up this new peace that came along with the acceptance that was seeping through her.

The relaxation couldn't be complete, though. It was too shot through with her awareness of Rob, of the light caress of his breath across her brow, the hard, confident strength of his encircling arm and the living reality of the body against which she was cradled. Unthinkingly she let her hand drop to his thigh; it came to rest high up, close to his groin, and the immediate tensing of the muscles beneath her fingers put flight to the healingly drifting mood that had held her.

'Who am I, Lucia?' he demanded in a low voice.

'You're Rob,' she answered him obediently, instinctively understanding why he needed to ask such a question.

'That's all right, then.'

He was turning and drawing her in to him, his lips seeking as she let her head fall back. Lucia was enveloped in warmth as she felt his mouth on hers and his hands roving about her body, the questing caresses openly seductive.

She was melting, all softness within, and he was hardness, his vibrant flesh and powerful muscles springing to rampant life under her eager hands.

Mouths ablaze with pleasure, their kisses grew increasingly passionate. Lucia felt engulfed by the passion, her blood singing and fizzing in her veins with erotic zest, and her fingers flew, unbuttoning his shirt, to find heated flesh and the tantalising tickle of his body hair for her palms' delight, and then for her lips too as he freed her mouth and she ducked her head swiftly to scatter wild, quick kisses all over his chest.

Her lips located the hard nub of one nipple and parted for her wayward tongue to linger delicately, tenderly stroking and teasingly flickering, and her senses rejoiced at the fierce ripple of response that ran through his body.

'That feels so good,' Rob murmured.

'*You* do,' she insisted shyly, smiling against him, almost mindless because this was the one thing that she and all humans could do without thought—find a mate, arouse and pleasure.

'And you're amazing,' he muttered, his lips brushing the smooth, polished skin beneath one ear as his fingers went skilfully about the task of unbuttoning her blouse.

She beat him to her bra, though, freeing her breasts to his touch, an almost soundless little cry of rapturous welcome escaping her as she felt his fingers close gently round one softly swollen mound.

Rob was easing her back to lie down, and she went willingly, careless of the sand that she would get in her hair because still she didn't want to be thinking yet. Feeling was sufficient; it was everything.

He was bent over her, a dark shape against the white dazzle of stars filling the jet-black sky, and her hands were urging him down to her. A swift, hard kiss for her silently beseeching mouth, and then he had left it, lips going on their sure way, travelling sensuously over her neck and one shoulder, and on to the stiff peak of the breast that his fingers still circled.

Then they moved to the other. Lucia's breasts felt unbelievably sensitive, tenderly aching, and as he took her fully into the hot moistness of his mouth her desire for him leapt incredibly and went on doing so, escalating unbearably. It was a raging, ravenous need that seemed to occupy her heart, or wherever her emotions had their fount, as much as the pulsing matrix of her womanhood. Her hands left his head and neck, her fingers biting frantically into his shoulders now as she surrendered to the frenzy devouring her.

Her hips were stirring urgently in obedience to the

piercing hunger deep within, lifting involuntarily in search of his maleness, and she moaned helplessly when Rob went still suddenly, his lips at rest in the hollow between her breasts.

Slowly he lifted his head, and she ventured shakily, 'Won't you. . .? Do you want to? Finish it? Make love, Rob?'

'No. Not yet,' he replied thoughtfully, moving away from her and sitting up, and a fine thread of humour laced his voice as he added, 'And certainly not out here. I don't think I want to be at one with nature to quite such an extent.'

She put out a hand to touch him. 'But—'

'Don't touch me for a minute, please, Lucia,' he cut in tautly, rising swiftly to his feet and turning his back on her.

Lucia twisted into a kneeling position. 'But what's wrong? Rob?' she demanded unevenly, utterly at a loss and beginning to be distressed.

'A whole lot,' he snapped harshly, and she saw him throw a glance back at her over his shoulder. 'Get up, Lucia! Get up at once!'

He sounded so furious suddenly, and so imperative that she scrambled to her feet in alarm, completely bewildered.

'Rob, what did I do?' she demanded anxiously, her voice thick with threatening tears.

'What was happening here was for all the wrong reasons—on both sides!' he asserted scathingly as he faced her. 'All right, I know you weren't using me as a substitute, but, judging by the confiding mood you were in a little while ago, it's comfort you're seeking tonight, and that's not a good enough reason for me. I don't make love to women to comfort them, to ease a broken heart—or to soothe a bruised ego!'

His words shocked her, and she strained to see his

expression in the darkness as he began fastening his shirt.

'But. . .'

Her voice faded away as she registered his tone. Humiliation scalded her. He had been showing kindess to her, but he wasn't prepared to take it beyond a certain point! Dear God, had she been imposing on him? Her face flamed, making her glad of the darkness.

'Accept it, Lucia. I don't think you're ready to take things further yet, which means I'm not ready either, and I may never be. Can you manage?' he added abruptly, seeing that she was struggling to disentangle her bra from her blouse.

'Yes!' Embarrassment made her voice clipped and emphatic.

She could guess what the wrong reason on his side had been. The need to pretend that he was involved with her was preventing anything developing between him and Madelon, or any of the other glamorous women around in whom he might have taken an interest, so he had probably been driven by simple frustration as much as by kindness or pity. *She* had been the substitute!

She was recalling the words he had used at first. 'Not yet.' He had been willing to indulge her with a few preliminaries to full lovemaking, and to indulge himself too—he must have been equally caught up in passion or he wouldn't have let it go so far—but, he was probably waiting before taking things any further, until he had decided how long he felt they needed to keep up the fiction in which they were engaged.

If it went on too long he might think it was worth going further, especially if he didn't feel that he could fairly go beyond mere flirtation with Madelon while ostensibly involved with another woman, but if they were to abandon the public pretence fairly soon then he wouldn't want the complication of a real entanglement.

Neither did she, Lucia reminded herself bleakly, so it was just as well that he had possessed the control to terminate the cycle of passion before it could complete itself. She didn't think she could cope with an affair based on sexual attraction. It would do too much damage to her self-respect, and how could she have forgotten that Rob himself had no emotional regard for her?

'All right?' Rob saw her fasten the last button of her blouse. 'Then come back to the hotel.'

'I apologise if I've. . .been imposing on you,' she offered stiffly as they started walking.

'You haven't.' He sounded slightly amused.

'I wasn't thinking properly,' she excused herself in a rush. 'That's what happens when you're so. . . Maybe you should go back to being all horrible and mocking. Then I'll behave normally.'

'I'm not sure if I can do that—unless you provoke me sufficiently, of course,' he qualified in a curiously regretful tone. 'You've needed the strength anger gives you, but you shouldn't any longer.'

'Don't patronise me,' Lucia snapped.

'Combustible Lucia! But I wasn't being patronising; I was merely stating what I know. Stop a moment; you've got sand all over you,' he informed her as they came within the flood of light streaming from the hotel building, and Lucia stood still and tense as he brushed gently at her hair and then the back of her shorts, emitting a breath of laughter as he did so. 'If anyone can see this they'll know exactly what we've been doing out on the beach.'

'Then at least from your point of view some good has come of it,' she quipped brightly as he finished and she turned to face him. 'After all, that's what our association is all about, isn't it?'

Rob studied her for several seconds without speaking, shadow making a mystery of his eyes.

Then he said, 'Anyone seeing your face will also know. Go in now, Lu. Goodnight.'

The abbreviation of her name startled her, because it ought to have denoted affection but that was the last thing he could possibly feel for her. Oh, it was probably just that Zimbabweans were as lazily casual in their speech as she had found their South African neighbours to be and shortened everything they could. Hadn't she once heard some of his compatriots referring to their country as 'Zims'?

A need to be out of his presence abruptly paramount, she obeyed with a curt nod, aware that he remained standing there, watching her go. Reaching her room in the staff annexe, she saw what he had meant by his reference to her face when she caught a glimpse of herself in the mirror. Attention arrested, she stared briefly before averting her gaze self-consciously.

Glittering eyes, blurred lips and flushed cheeks all proclaimed exactly what he had said they did, and even when this outward evidence had faded an inner disturbance remained, encroaching relentlessly on her mind, troubling her while she was awake and fretting at her dreams.

It was still present the next day too, pushing its way forward whenever she had a moment to spare from the demands and distractions of her job. Lucia was afraid of her thoughts now, with a feeling that she was incubating some item of knowledge that would cease being inchoate and emerge absolute, exact and unalterable if she gave too much time to nurturing it.

Thus she welcomed every customer to the hotel shop, especially those who were disposed to linger and chat. She didn't want to have to give mental space to anything personal, least of all the way Rob had made her feel and the unwelcome truths it seemed to presuppose.

At least she saw nothing of him all day, but out of sight definitely didn't mean out of mind in this case.

Even Thierry Olivier, waiting for her after she'd left the shop in the care of the Comorean teenager who looked after it during the evenings, was to be seized on as a useful distraction from thought, if nothing else.

'We haven't really had a chance to talk properly,' he ventured longingly as she looked at him enquiringly.

'I thought we said everything relevant the other evening,' Lucia responded a little tartly. 'I know I did, especially now I've met your Nadine. Did she tell you she'd been to see me? I'm sure you'll be very happy together. When's the wedding?'

'I'm not sure. We're still deciding,' Thierry replied; he paused and rushed on anxiously, 'Lucia, you must tell me. Am I doing right to be marrying her?'

To her surprise her initial reaction was to feel a prickle of irritation, and she sighed sharply.

'Thierry, you've got Nadine now.' She tried to speak gently. 'You have to get out of the habit of expecting me to make up your mind for you. That's all it is, and you know something? You're already sure she's the right woman for you or you couldn't have brought yourself to the point of getting engaged to her and running the risk of having to face all sorts of unpleasantness when she and I found out about each other, although I know you must have been hoping that somehow that side of it would just go away. But think about it. *You* made the decision.'

'Yes, I did!' Thierry sounded more confident. 'I had got into the habit of waiting for you to decide things for us, but when I met her I found I knew my own mind again... But you are still good for me, Lucia— the way you make me look at things.'

She gave him a quick, happy smile as she remembered, 'I've still got our ring. You'd better come and get it now. It's in my room in staff quarters.'

She hadn't put the ring in the hotel safe, mainly because she had shrunk from the idea of some entirely unlikely breach of security by which word might get out about her deposit, causing people who knew her, such as Hassan Mohammed, to realise that she had returned to the Comoros believing herself still engaged to Thierry.

She would give him the ring now, and then her freedom would be absolute.

Lucia's blue-green eyes went blank as the thought finally forced her to confront the revelation she had been first fumbling for and then dodging.

She didn't love Thierry, and she hadn't done so for quite some time. Worse, she didn't think she had ever loved him in the way a woman should love the man she was going to marry.

CHAPTER EIGHT

'WHAT about you?' Thierry questioned Lucia when they were in her room. 'You and Rob Ballard? You're not serious about him? Nadine says she thinks he may never marry, and for you. . . He is so harsh.'

Lucia managed a brilliant, dismissive smile as she turned to face him, holding out the ring.

'Harsh by your standards, I know. No, of course I'm not serious.' She laughed as she dropped the shining circle of gold with its glittering stone into the hand he extended. 'I think you kept the little case it came in, didn't you?

'I'm just having fun right now, Thierry, enjoying my freedom. We were together too young, weren't we? Too young for me, I mean; and we were so close and so comfortable that we became a habit with each other, I think, drifting along and never bothering to examine ourselves. We both needed these Ballards dropping into our lives and waking us up.'

There was no need to hurt him by telling him that she had allowed a need for the security of being settled, of belonging, to persuade her that affection and a youthful, superficial attraction were love. Let him believe that she had truly loved him and stopped.

'Then you have no regrets?'

Thierry looked and sounded wistful, standing there hesitating as she opened the door for him, and Lucia felt impatient. He had Nadine. What more did he want?

'None. We've had some good moments over the years, and I think you probably did me one immense favour, because having you in my life kept me on the straight and narrow at varsity instead of throwing myself into the social side of campus life. It can be a sexual funfair, and I might have been distracted to the detriment of my studies and have ended up breaking my promise to my father if I'd failed and somehow not been able to either sit retakes or repeat a year.'

Realising that it probably wasn't what he wanted to hear, she pushed him gently out into the wide, carpeted corridor and added affectionately, 'I'll always be fond of you, Thierry.'

Trite though it was, she realised that it was the strict truth as she hugged him and felt him put his arms round her.

'And I of you,' he responded emotionally, but then she felt him stiffen.

Raising her head, she saw Rob striding towards them from the far end of the corridor where the resident staff's private lounge was situated. Presumably he was in search of her, although not necessarily, as Madelon Brouard occupied the room next to hers.

'There's an exit the other way,' she whispered to Thierry, urging him in the opposite direction as a last act of kindness to him, knowing that he was thinking about what Rob might say to Nadine about this. He went with alacrity, leaving her to turn and call impulsively, 'Rob?'

There was nothing enigmatic about his eyes as he reached her. They were blazing with anger, and the same emotion was hardening his face and imparting a tight, ruthless curve to his lips.

'Protecting your lover, Lucia?' he taunted with unconcealed disgust. 'But it's not me he'll have to face. It's my sister. And he's not going to slide surreptitiously out of that engagement the way he did with the other.'

'He's not—'

'How long have you had him in here with you?' he swept on contemptuously. 'Long enough for you to effect a reconciliation, anyway, going by the touching leave-taking I've just witnessed. I came in the way you've just sent him out—I thought I'd see if you were in the staff lounge first, before I tried your room.

'I should have known you'd have a crack at getting him back. You've implied that you might try often enough, but I was inclined to think it was the wrong side of pride prompting you, and that you had the intelligence to be looking at it from the right angle by now and wouldn't have him back on any terms.'

'Nothing happened; I wasn't trying to get him back,' Lucia protested with furious indignation, her hands giving agitated emphasis to the denial.

'Spare me the lies even if you must persist in lying to yourself,' Rob snapped. 'This door was closed when I passed. Why was the door closed if it was so innocent?'

'I don't know! Habit—like I told him everything else was,' she suggested bitingly.

'I'm really not that interested in what you told each other, Lucia,' he retorted caustically.

'Listen to me, damn it!' Her voice rose.

'I think what I despise most about you is the damage you're prepared to do to yourself for him,' Rob offered savagely, beginning to turn away from her. 'Not forgetting the damage to him. And I don't feel like standing here listening to you deceiving yourself, and trying to convince me that you won't be making any sacrifices for him, when the only real reason you've made the effort to get him back in the first place is because you can't face up to the fact that another woman suits him better than you.

'I suppose you had to use sex to persuade him it's you he wants after all. Well, you're good there, I'll grant you that.'

It was so insulting that sheer temper held her silent for several seconds. Then she realised that he was walking away from her.

'Come back! Don't you call me a liar and then walk away from me,' she raged imperiously. 'You're supposed to know me—understand me—so you should know if I'm lying or not!'

It succeeded in halting his departure. He stood so still that he seemed to have been mentally arrested as well, and she saw the alert, oddly intent angle at which he held his head, as if he was concentrating on something, or, perhaps, waiting for more.

But she was incapable of further speech for the moment, possessed by a sense of some self-betrayal. Why should she care if he believed her or not? But she did; she needed him to.

He was turning slowly and retracing his steps, his expression curiously questioning as he searched the angry confusion in her eyes.

'That's quite a challenge, and perhaps you're right,' he acknowledged softly.

'So do you—?'

She stopped, aware of the door to the next room opening and Madelon looking out, grinning meaningfully at them and retreating.

'Go inside.' Rob urged Lucia gently into her own room with him and closed the door.

The contact was brief—just the slightest pressure of his hand on her shoulder, felt through the fine cotton of her short, straight melon-pink shift—but it sent her hurtling back to the mind-fazing physical awareness of him that had possessed her last night. Lucia swallowed, realising that she had probably made a mistake in not letting him just walk away.

'I was. . .I gave Thierry his ring back,' she explained haltingly, meeting his eyes warily. 'That's why he was in here.'

'Yes?' He paused, absorbing it. 'And what else?'

'So obviously I wasn't trying to get him back!' she snapped resentfully. 'You should know that! You talk

about my. . .my pride often enough, and you're right!
Whatever I feel or don't feel for Thierry, I wouldn't
have him back on any terms, damn it!'

'That's the intelligent attitude,' he commended her
sardonically.

'And, if you must know, I agree with you that Nadine
suits him better than I would,' Lucia added tempestuously. 'I'm. . .I was bad for him.'

And that was quite enough, she decided, silencing
herself. She wasn't about to tell him about the discovery she had just made concerning her feelings for
Thierry. He would only be derisive, or contemptuous.
Of course, he would realise sooner or later, if they had
much more to do with each other, just as he guessed
everything else she was feeling, but he could work at
grasping something for once!

'So, even if you're still hurt by what he has done, you
should be able to be philosophical about it for his sake
and reflect that he has had a narrow escape,' Rob
suggested brutally. 'If not for Nadine, you might have
been married with babies before you'd realised that,
martyring yourself and trying to make the best of things
for everyone's sake.'

Lucia stared at him, her sensitive imagination cring-
ing before the awfulness of the situation that she might
have created.

Then, without any warning, the emotional resilience
that had enabled her to meet the demands of the last
few days buckled fatally, and Lucia burst into tears, not
so much in relief as in reaction to her own stupidity.

'I still feel such a fool!' she gulped by way of excuse,
although it was part of the truth too. 'I feel. . .
humiliated!'

'Most people would, and especially anyone with
pride as sensitive as yours,' Rob suggested dismissively,
reaching for her.

The embarrassment she was experiencing at finding

herself crying in front of him was compounded by the all too obvious reluctance with which he drew her to him. Lucia didn't just sense it; she literally felt it in the slow, unwilling way his arm curved about her shoulders.

'And I'm making a total fool of myself again now,' she sobbed stormily, unable to stop the tears yet, despite her shamed awareness that she was forcing him into a position that he clearly found distasteful—having to offer comfort.

'Not that.' The long fingers cupping the back of her head as he pressed it into his shoulder were also reluctant. 'You haven't let anyone else guess what you're going through. You've stayed and faced both Olivier and Nadine on a couple of occasions instead of running away and hiding, which is what a lot of people would do under similar circumstances.'

'I was only able to do it because I was so angry,' she said tempestuously.

'I know.'

Even his voice was reluctant, and it was that which finally enabled Lucia to stop crying. She lifted her head and glared at him with furious, tear-drenched eyes.

'You don't really want to be here. . .doing this, do you?' she accused unevenly, and Rob looked back at her with the faintest of sardonic smiles flickering about his mouth.

'No, not really,' he agreed coolly after a few seconds, letting her go as she took a step backwards. 'For various reasons.'

'Well, you don't have to! I'm only using you,' Lucia asserted defiantly, suddenly desperate to give the appearance of strength as a counter to the shaming weakness she had revealed.

'The same way you were last night—for comfort?' Pausing, he considered the claim. 'Yes, I suppose we could say that. You will get over Olivier in time, you know, Lucia.'

She knew that had she been truly in love with Thierry, and suffering over his betrayal, she might have challenged this prediction, pointing out that, after all, he hadn't got over his Shelagh. But it would have been cruel to taunt him with that now when she was so much better off than he, free because she hadn't truly loved Thierry, whereas he was bound for ever, it seemed, to a woman with whom he couldn't live.

So she merely said lightly, 'Is that one more thing you're going to be right about?'

'I know you find it hard to believe at present, but all the signs of recovery are there already,' Rob retorted, with a glint of something very like disgust in his eyes.

'Sorry to have...burdened you, being a baby and all,' Lucia began stiltedly, and then proper anger was restored. 'It's your own fault, though. If you didn't... see me, see into me the way you do, I wouldn't have felt I could.'

'In other words, knowing how you work places me under some sort of obligation to you?' Rob mocked silkily.

She was dismayed to realise that she had indeed been thinking, or feeling, along those lines, and the knowledge that he was unwilling to accept any such obligation was unexpectedly hurtful. But how had she gone from resenting the way he knew her so accurately to unthinking reliance on the same ability?

'I realise it was...an imposition, and I apologise.' She spoke with a proud little lift of her chin, depriving her words of anything approaching humility.

'No problem,' Rob returned lightly.

'Why were you looking for me?' Lucia changed the subject, resisting an urge to rub at her damp cheeks with the back of her hand.

'To suggest that we had dinner together tonight,' he supplied blandly.

'Oh, but—' Lucia was shocked by the weight of the

disappointment that sank into her as she realised something else. 'That act isn't really necessary any more, is it, Rob? I've just told you that I don't want Thierry back, so you must be sure I've got no intention of coming between him and your sister. Nadine is already sure of that—you can ask her if you like—and that's what the whole thing has been about, her peace of mind. It was never for me.'

'Except that it seems to have been after all.' Rob paused, examining her assessingly. 'But we could still have dinner together, simply because we want to.'

Lucia hesitated, tempted. After all, what better way was there to celebrate her belatedly discovered freedom than by spending an hour or so in the company of probably the most attractive and sexy man she had ever met? Of course, he wouldn't know that it was a private celebration.

'*Do* you want to?' She was wary, remembering his reluctant attitude when she had been crying. 'Wouldn't you prefer Madelon? She's together—not messed up or mixed up like me.'

'No, you.' Sudden laughter lit his face, increasing its attractiveness irresistibly. 'And why are you being so cautious? It's only dinner we're discussing here, not a whole relationship. Yes or no, Lucia? Quickly, because you're probably breaking some kind of staff rule by having me in here.'

'You're the boss; you're Ballard; you can do what you like,' she retorted, and he laughed again.

'Be careful, Lucia, I might misunderstand you.'

'Except that you never do,' she retorted in a dry little voice. 'All right, yes to dinner. Where shall I meet you?'

She wasn't sure why she had agreed, but she was denied an immediate opportunity to think about it, or anything else, because Madelon Brouard knocked softly on her door a few minutes after Rob had gone.

'All is well again?' she enquired, entering the room in response to Lucia's bidding after identifying herself. 'You will forgive my curiosity, please, but lovers' quarrels are intriguing, and you understand that I have this interest in Rob for myself. I was aware of a fracas when I looked out earlier.'

Lucia laughed. 'I had something of Thierry Olivier's from way back that I wanted to return, and Rob was annoyed at finding him here.'

'Possessiveness, or jealousy,' Madelon decided sagely, and shrugged philosophically. 'If the affair is so exciting and intense—but no! You cannot give check-mate to me yet, my friend! He knows I pursue him and he does not reject my interest.'

She was funny, and Lucia liked her, so why was she beginning to be disturbed by her periodic references to winning Rob for herself?

Later Lucia changed into a pretty dress, its small black and white print, the lace-edged sweetheart neckline and the way it fitted over her breasts, waist and hips before falling in soft folds to her knees, all ultra-feminine.

'Nice,' Rob commented when she met him at the restaurant, but there was no kiss for show this time. Lucia was relieved, suddenly at the mercy of an acute physical awareness which shafted through her and set up an atrocious longing deep inside her.

He himself was elegant, as always, in casually smart trousers and a slate-coloured shirt, but it was the man, not the clothes producing this debilitating effect on her—things such as the midnight darkness of his hair, the power and magnetism of character so evident in his face, the enigma of his eyes, the shapely strength and beauty of his hands and, above all, the mysterious mouth that could express so much.

'We have a few matters to get out of the way,' he

announced decisively when they were seated at an attractively laid table at the open end of the restaurant. 'First, I neglected to mention earlier that I spoke to my sister today. She was talking about my having dinner at the Olivier place again on Friday night, and she was wondering how you'd feel about an invitation. Madame Olivier isn't being given a say, if you're wondering.'

'I'd rather not,' Lucia decided finally, flushing self-consciously. 'Thierry seems a bit. . .wistful still when he's around me, so it will probably be better for both of them if I keep away. He'll become comfortable and confident with Nadine quicker if he isn't always remembering how comfortable he used to be with me. Oh, I know how conceited this sounds, but it's true. I know him.'

He touched her hand, which was typically busy, playing tensely with her knife.

'It sounds considerate,' he contradicted her gently. 'All right, I'll tell Nadine we can't make it.'

'Oh, but you must go,' Lucia insisted quickly, embarrassed. 'I didn't mean to deprive you. . . You've done enough, even if it was all meant for Nadine. She doesn't need the act any longer, and I don't need any more face-saving. . .rescuing.'

'*You* will be rescuing *me* on this occasion,' he retorted humorously. 'I'm fond of my sister but we're not that close, and we'll be even less so once I've seen her safely married, because that will be the long-overdue end of my responsibility for her.

'But I am definitely not pining to spend another evening over there, listening to Madame Olivier politely mourning the good old days before the Ballard Group and other hotel chains created employment and brought in the tourists and their foreign currency.'

'I'm sure you give as good as you get,' Lucia laughed, relieved to realise that he was sincere.

'When I want to, and when the criticism might be

valid, but I've never seen the need to defend myself against uninformed condemnation. The wedding, now, Lucia. Do you go on the guest list?' Rob went on.

'When and where are they getting married anyway? Thierry said they hadn't decided yet.'

'I know. Soon, Nadine says, but they're still weighing the Comoros against Harare—I suppose because it's traditional for weddings to take place from the bride's home.' Rob sounded indifferent.

'Well, if it's Zimbabwe and soon, that settles the question of my presence. I won't be able to afford it even if I get an invitation.'

'Presumably you'll be saving with the aim of leaving the islands in due time? What do you think you'll do then?'

Lucia's eyes began to sparkle as she realised that she had choices.

'Anything I like! It has just occurred to me!' She finally grasped at her freedom and embraced it. 'The time I'll have to spend here will be beneficial, as it'll enable me to find out if I really like hotel work. If I do, I'll stay with it in some form; otherwise I might try to get into some line of personnel work, always depending on where I go and what opportunities exist.'

'So, essentially, the world is your oyster.' The mockery that had been in abeyance for a while was back, and a challenging smile twisted his lips. 'You've kept your promise to your father, you haven't been called on to keep the one you made to Thierry Olivier— although I don't suppose you're ready to count that as a blessing yet—and you're no longer anyone's puppet.'

His tone doused her pleasure.

'A freedom which you've given some attention to trying to show me I could and should always have had,' she reminded him sharply.

'I have, haven't I?' he conceded ironically.

'So why—' Lucia broke off as realisation hit her, and

she sent him a taunting smile. 'Oh, I know! It's nothing personal, and yet very personal to you at the same time, isn't it? I'd forgotten. I was talking about possible careers, and you simply don't like women who are madly dedicated to their work—because of your mother and that woman Nadine told me about.'

'What woman?' Rob demanded.

'I shouldn't have mentioned her,' she realised contritely.

'Shelagh, I suppose?' he prompted resignedly.

'I think so. Someone who researched monkeys or baboons,' she admitted.

'Chimpanzees and gorillas,' he corrected her flatly.

'It was insensitive of me to raise the subject. You probably didn't want to be reminded,' she guessed, and he smiled ironically.

'But you're *sensitive*, Lucia,' he contradicted her, his eyes gleaming. 'Only your concern is superfluous here, angel. I made a mistake, but I'm not particularly touchy about it. My experience with Shelagh taught me a valuable lesson about myself. I wanted all her time, attention, presence and energy, but her absorption in her work took her away a lot, only allowing her to reserve a portion of them for me, so in the end I decided against forming what she would have termed a "pair-bond".'

'It must have hurt, though,' Lucia ventured quietly.

'I suppose it did. It was my first seriously emotional affair, and it taught me what sort of women to avoid for future relationships.'

Lucia understood. It had also been his *only* seriously emotional affair, so he had never got over Shelagh, and this hard, almost careless attitude was his way of coping with the pain.

Aware of being luckier than Rob, in that her heart was free, she guessed that he'd prefer a less serious note, and she obliged by asking lightly, 'Doesn't it

worry you that a lot of people might call you reactionary and sexist?'

'No, because I'm not those things,' he returned
bluntly, the denial inherently arrogant. 'I'm possessive
and demanding. Those are traits in my personal make-
up, not the attitudes of ignorant prejudice.'

'Flaws in your personal make-up,' she jibed.

'Yes.'

Lucia was awed. How could he admit it so easily?
Compared with her over-sensitivity about herself and
her faults, she supposed his acceptance and admission
of his revealed how comfortable he was with himself—
secure and confident.

'You could have tried overcoming them,' she suggested sweetly.

'I may yet have to,' he responded rather grimly.

Because the fact that no one had succeeded in
replacing Shelagh was forcing him to consider the
possibility of resuming the relationship? Lucia found
the idea unexpectedly disturbing.

'Why haven't you before? For instance,' she continued mischievously, 'if this ape-woman was so
devoted to her work, why didn't you just give up yours
and follow her, so you could be be with her all the
time? Or is the idea too progressive for you?'

The challenge restored a glint of humour to the
smoky eyes. 'It's the idea of any inborn talent going to
waste that is anathema to me. Shelagh has a talent for
what she does; I happen to have a talent for what I do;
therefore we were incompatible, as the natural possession of a particular ability would seem to indicate
that it's intended for use. I don't quarrel with destiny.'

Rob treated her to a long, searching inspection
before resuming, 'And you have a talent for getting on
with people, although no one would ever guess it if
they had only your dealings with me these past few
days to go on. I wonder what you're destined to end up

doing? How are you liking being in the hotel shop so far?'

It all seemed oddly intent, more than merely a concession to social conversation, but Lucia answered him amicably, her mind playing over some of the things he had been saying.

She didn't think that she could ever devote herself as exclusively to any career as Jacynth Cole-Ballard and Shelagh seemed to have done, but then what Rob had called 'talent' was actually genius in the former's case— and probably in Shelagh's too. Her own talent rested on a more humbly human level, unrelated to any specific subject. The sort of work that suited her temperament and abilities would provide stimulation and fulfilment, but ultimately she required the warmth of a personal relationship to give fundamental meaning to her life.

So she would be needing someone to love some day, but would anyone love her properly? Thierry hadn't gone on loving her, but maybe that was because she hadn't loved him enough. Oh, she hoped that she didn't make any more mistakes!

Over their meal Lucia told Rob about Chester Watson's approval of some plans for the shop.

'I've got tomorrow morning off to go to Moroni to get what we'll need—some of those big round baskets, vanilla sticks, the various spices. . .oh, everything! The informative literature we sell looks boring just stacked by itself, but we can turn it into an attractive display around examples of the islands' more exotic products. Hassan has suggested that we also have a small display in the reception area, and Chester thinks it's a good idea.'

'"We",' Rob echoed reflectively. 'You're really getting into this, aren't you, identifying with the hotel?'

'That's what I like about working in a hotel; we can

be united because we've all got the same aim—to please.'

'As long as you don't carry the desire to the extremes you do in your personal life,' he cautioned her, his expression inscrutable.

'Oh, that's all over and done with.' Lucia was blithely dismissive. 'I told you days ago—I'm through with pleasing men!'

'It's those you love who inspire you to near-martyr-dom, isn't it?' Rob probed tautly.

'I suppose. . .' Now she sounded uncertain.

'So you'd better not let yourself love anyone again once you get over Olivier, right?' he pursued relentlessly.

'No.' She spoke flatly, because she didn't think she possessed that much cool self-control.

He directed the conversation towards impersonal areas after that, but the little exchange had left her harbouring a feeling of unidentifiable distress, and a strange restlessness had begun to gnaw at her.

Rob walked her back to the staff annexe when the meal was over. Although some part of her had been half-expecting it, he made no attempt to touch her, and Lucia was conscious of shaming disappointment.

What was wrong with her? She ought to be glad and grateful as it seemed that she was incapable of control-ling her hormones, or whatever it was that made her so physically responsive to him. The last thing she wanted was to find herself helplessly caught up in an affair based purely on sex. That would constitute an even worse mistake than the one she had made with Thierry.

Lucia had thought she might lie awake, relishing the prospect of the freedom that she had finally discovered she had, but somehow it had lost its taste. Instead she was plagued by an obscurely dissatisfied feeling, which she didn't think had much to do with her libido because it troubled her more as a sense of something being missing from her emotional life than from her physical existence.

Maybe just the habit of Thierry, she decided, but remained dubious about the explanation.

She slept eventually and woke unable to remember what she had dreamed. Her feeling of dissatisfaction hardened into the frustration which came of knowing that something had been forgotten and would remain so if effort was expended on trying to remember.

Covering up was merely optional, even for Muslims in the Comoros, so, when Lucia stepped outside to look for the car that Chester had told her she could use to go to Moroni, she was wearing a short red divided skirt and matching button-up top with a pin-tucked yoke, both in soft, fine cotton.

An earlier squall had yielded to one of those mornings when the sun was at its most relentlessly scorching, burning tender skins through a shimmering haze of heat, so she had added a natural straw hat and her sunglasses, with lightweight leather sandals and a hand-woven shoulder bag from South Africa completing the outfit.

'This is the car you're looking for.'

She just managed to prevent herself colliding with Rob, and saw that he was indicating the car in which he had driven her to collect her luggage from the Olivier estate the previous Saturday. Madelon was with him and she gave Lucia an insouciant smile.

'Enjoy!' she adjured, and disappeared into the hotel.

Her manner struck Lucia as being both challenging and triumphant, so perhaps Rob had finally been explicitly encouraging. Lucia frowned. Would he do that, though—indulge his obvious interest in Madelon and risk giving the lie to his pretended interest in *her*?

Of course, he was so clever that he might have found

a way that eliminated any risk. She didn't know Madelon well enough to be sure if she would go along with a subterfuge or demand to be allowed to flaunt her triumph. But he could only be playing with Madelon, if Shelagh was still the woman he loved.

'Chester said a Fiat,' she protested distractedly to Rob, her breathing erratic and her heart still drumming painfully with shock—just because she hadn't been expecting to see him.

'That was when he thought you were going on your own. I'm going with you,' he announced smoothly.

'Oh. . .but why?' Lucia was still disconcerted.

'Why wouldn't I want to spend the morning with a girlfriend—of sorts—when my schedule has left me a few hours free?'

'I'm not a girlfriend of *any* sort,' she snapped, beginning to recover her fighting spirit.

'Let's say a female companion, then.' Rob was clearly in an easygoing mood, smiling lazily. 'My favourite way of relaxing.'

'Did Madelon turn you down?'

'I didn't ask her.'

'I suppose you felt you couldn't when you haven't had a chance to do anything about her because that stupid act of ours has taken up your time,' she derided. 'You can't think it's still necessary?'

'Because you don't want Olivier back? I know it's not,' he drawled.

Lucia shrugged and smiled, moving towards the car with him. Warmth was stealing into her heart and softening it as she accepted that he at least found her company preferable to none at all.

'Let's go, then, Rob. I suppose I owe you, as it's partly due to me that you haven't had the opportunity to get acquainted with a more appropriate woman,' she quipped as he opened the door for her, and he was still laughing when he came round to the driver's side and got into the car.

From behind dark lenses she watched his lean fingers insert the ignition key and turn it, and observed his denim-encased legs flex slightly as he tested the pedals. Then she transferred her gaze to his nearest arm, taut and brown below the sleeve of a casual oatmeal-coloured shirt, his muscles rippling subtly beneath the burnished skin as he put the car into gear.

She swallowed emotionally, resisting a compulsion to reach out and touch, or lean forward and press her lips to that firm, tanned flesh.

Why had she needed to sound as if she was making some grudging concession in agreeing to go to Moroni with him? She would do anything for him.

She loved him so much.

CHAPTER NINE

How had it happened?

Lucia was shaking violently under the impact of the disaster that had befallen her. She had never been so grateful for her sunglasses, and Rob's silence as he concentrated on easing the car towards the main road was the only other mercy granted to her.

Her lips were trembling uncontrollably and her hands had made frantic contact with each other in front of her, fingers lacing tensely then beginning to writhe agitatedly.

Inevitably, Rob noticed.

'What's wrong?'

'I've just—Nothing!' Face flaming, she stopped herself blurting it out just in time.

'Something you need? Shall we turn back?' he offered considerately.

The sensitivity of that almost made her weep, and it was a moment or two before she could find her voice.

'No! I'm fine. Just don't. . .don't talk to me for a bit, please,' she requested thickly.

He moved his head briefly in acknowledgement and put out his hand, touching her thigh in reassurance.

'Or touch you either,' he accepted sardonically, taking his hand away as he felt the clenching increase of her tension.

For the first time Lucia was afraid of him. He knew her so well. How could he not know this? Or, knowing, did he feel even more contempt or pity than he already had?

She stole a quick glance at Rob. She had never dreamed that she could feel so much pain, and this whole thing was loaded with yet more potential pain. If he realised, he might even find it funny, when less than a week ago she had still believed that she was in love with Thierry.

Lucia had no problem with that aspect herself, now that she understood that the boy-and-girl affair with Thierry must have run its sweet course long ago. Her mistake had been to be tempted by the prospect of having somewhere to belong at last, to be prepared to offer succour and protection, letting him depend on her in return for that.

But her apparent fickleness could easily prove to be a source of amusement to Rob. She didn't know which she would hate most from him—pity, derision or contempt.

Lucia's fingers continued their desperate wrestling with each other. Everyone she had ever loved before, in whatever way—Thierry, parents, friends—had loved her in return, to a greater or lesser degree—if only temporarily in Thierry's case. She just didn't know what to do with this unreciprocated love, especially when it was so much greater than any other she had known. This was a love for a lifetime. She recognised it with unshakeable, bone-deep certainty, and yet there was so little that Rob might want of her, and nothing at all that he needed.

Anger, resentment and even much of her pride were obliterated now, because love was stronger than them all. Typically, she ached to express it by securing his happiness for him. She would do, be and give anything he asked of her, and the real agony lay in knowing how pitifully little he would ever ask.

Some pride remained, because she didn't think that she wanted him knowing she loved him, although she was forced to accept the possibility that he would do so sooner or later, just because he understood her so perfectly.

But maybe she could go about the business of loving him in secret for a while. Her hands dropped passively into her lap as she made the commitment, and she sighed, accepting her fate together with the longing and anguish it dictated.

'All right?' Rob enquired, obviously sensitive to her altered mood.

'Fine!'

Lucia gave him her sunniest smile, the love-hunger in her eyes hidden by her dark glasses, and set about loving him.

Her sole desire was to please, her voluntary task to study and indulge his mood, his every whim. There could be no self-abnegation or hypocrisy in doing so, because his pleasure was now hers.

She responded enthusiastically to every topic he chose to introduce, and, loving him, found herself at last understanding him and consequently loving him even more, because this was no man to demand either a docilely admiring audience or mindless agreement. She was free to argue if she disagreed, and she did so with a grace and humour that she had not shown him before.

In Moroni, the Comorean archipelago's tiny capital, with its mosques giving it an intrinsically Islamic atmosphere, reminiscent of Zanzibar and other such historical centres of commerce in the trade-winds zone, she fell in happily with his suggestion that they stroll around the white-walled harbour before going up to the market-place.

'When you're in a good mood, you really sparkle, don't you?' Rob commented teasingly when they paused and she removed her hat as she leaned against the wall, face ostensibly lifted to the sun, although in reality she was adoring him with her concealed eyes.

'This is the real me,' she quipped, her sensitive

mouth breaking into a scintillating smile of delight because he was pleased with her.

He produced a slow smile of his own.

'And it charms—especially your mind, like a star... or a magnum, full of champagne thoughts to go with the champagne smiles.' He paused before adding in a slightly harder voice, 'But I think I'm glad I can't see what you're hiding behind those shades. Put your hat on again too, Lu, or you'll burn.'

He was close to knowing, she guessed, and found herself wishing—praying—that she might be granted today simply to love him before she had to be embarrassed by his knowing and before pride's need to find some dignified way of dealing with it perhaps made her prickly and self-conscious in his company.

When she had spent most of the money with which Chester Watson had instructed his assistant to provide her in the colourful, essentially Third-World market-place, Rob ascertained how much time she had before she had to be back on duty and then drove her to lunch at an elegant hotel just outside Moroni.

They ate inside, so Lucia was forced to remove her sunglasses, but she thought it could do no harm now that she knew it was for his sake that she needed to hide what she was feeling. Anything that was in Rob's interests was easy, and it had occurred to her that he wouldn't *want* to know that she loved him any more than *she* wanted him to.

Over their meal she witnessed the professional side of Rob, aware of his clever eyes noting everything— layout, decor, service and more—and she knew that he was comparing this hotel, part of a famous chain, with those in the Ballard Group.

'Our hotel is much better,' she volunteered sincerely, and he laughed with a real appreciation that lit his entire face, bringing a tender smile of satisfaction to her lips.

'Of course it is.'

'Because it's a Ballard one,' she responded lyrically, and his smile became complicated.

'At last I'm getting to see the sunny-natured girl Hassan Mohammed described to me.' The smile faded and he sounded curiously intense as he asked, 'Have you simply found a new brand of courage, or are you really so happy all of a sudden, Lucia?'

'Oh, yes,' she assured him, ambiguously, and he looked slightly sceptical.

She was as happy as she was ever going to be, she reflected, hiding the seeping sadness the thought occasioned—and that was half-happy, and only if Rob was happy. For her to be wholly happy, he would have to love her.

'And free?' His voice still had that imperative tone, almost urgent now. 'Or just accepting?'

'Free too,' she managed composedly.

She supposed she was—free to love him. She didn't want any other freedom. She wanted him to imprison her in his love. He had confessed to being demanding and possessive in his relationships. She wanted to be the one chosen to meet his demands and submit to the possessiveness. There would be no shame in such a surrender, nothing to bruise her pride, because if he loved her it would automatically mean that he respected her.

But how could he?

'I just hope you mean it,' Rob was responding, with an odd inflexion in his voice, and she saw an expression of reserve take hold of his face, hardening it until the skin seemed to be stretched over unyielding steel.

Don't let him know yet.

The wish was so fervent that it wrenched at her heart, and Lucia threw herself into the business of pleasing once more, a little sigh of relief rushing from her lungs as he co-operatively gauged her mood and responded to it.

Impersonal subjects were the rule for the remainder of the meal, and as they drove back along the coast afterwards.

'Thank you, Rob,' Lucia said when she was out of the car, keeping her hands curled into fists at her sides in resistance to an impulse to reach out and pull him towards her.

'It was an absolute pleasure, Lucia,' he returned amusedly, handing her her purchases. 'Don't forget we're having dinner tomorrow night. Tonight is out, unfortunately. I've got a formal working dinner with some members of the government. They're far from being fundamentalists, but it's a strictly male affair, nevertheless.

'I'm going to have to spend most of tomorrow with Chester Watson and the senior admin staff, but I'll find time to let you know where and when. All right?'

If he was going to be that busy, at least she wouldn't have to torture herself by imagining him with Madelon when he wasn't around!

Rob came into the hotel shop early the following evening, giving her a quick smile and waiting patiently while she concluded a transaction.

'Rob?' she greeted him questioningly when the couple departed after she had confirmed that they had made the right choice of sunscreen for their toddler's peachy skin.

'Tonight? Will you come up to my suite around eight-thirty and we'll have dinner there?' He waited a moment, to see if she raised any objections and, observing her beginning to nod and smile, continued, 'I'll see you then. Right now I'm supposed to be hosting a session at the pool bar with Chester and the others who've worked with us today. Don't worry, I won't get

drunk—although they're entitled to if that's their inclination after all their input.'

He departed, but before he had gone very far she
saw Madelon approach him, and he stopped to talk to
her for a few seconds, the sound of their mingled
laughter intensifying the ache in Lucia's heart.

'She didn't know if he understood Madelon as well
as he did her or not, but, even if he did, he would like
and respect her. Madelon wasn't a mixed-up mess of a
person as she was; she didn't take love or sex too
seriously, and she didn't make stupid mistakes in her
personal life.

Lucia knew better than to believe that there was any
significance at all in his decision that they should have
dinner in his suite. After working hard all day, he
probably simply didn't feel like having to make himself
charming to the sort of strangers who couldn't be
satisfied with just recognising a public figure but had to
approach and attempt to engage him in conversation.

Yet she couldn't help remembering the phrases that
he had used on the beach the other night: 'not yet' had
been his reply when she had asked if he wanted to
make love, and he had talked of their not being
ready. . .

Oh, she was being stupid to think that he had been
doing anything more than letting her down gently. He
was attracted to Madelon, and he loved Shelagh.

Anyway, from Rob's point of view nothing had
changed since that night, except that he was now
confident that she wasn't going to try and win Thierry
back. That was hardly enough to persuade him that she
was now ready, always supposing that he had given any
subsequent thought at all to the feeling that had flared
between them out there on the beach.

But he *might* want to take things further. Lucia's
heart raced as she contemplated the possibility. It had
to be Rob's decision. She knew that she couldn't set

out to seduce him, or even make her desire for him too obvious. To do so might be to impose, and perhaps sway him towards something he might not otherwise choose.

Nevertheless, she showered and dressed herself with all the care of the bride on her wedding day when the time came to start readying herself to go to Rob's suite.

The dress she chose—straight and simple—was a deep, subtle shade of dark green which lent depth to the colour of her eyes, while her dangling earrings were in several shades of brighter green; they were the tiny, exquisitely wrought birds which had suddenly appeared and become fashionable in several southern African countries in recent years. Her straight hair shone and the lipstick she kept for special occasions—a soft, tawny red— imparted a satiny sheen to her sensitive lips.

She wished that she had some scent, but the need to save for her returning trips to the Comoros had precluded such luxuries, and Madelon wasn't around to borrow from, so she went up to Rob's suite unperfumed save for the faint fragrance of her newly washed hair.

'You look gorgeous,' he complimented her, with a quick flashing smile, when she arrived, but there was such a strange, hard light in his eyes that she was dismayed.

His choice of neutral topics of conversation while they had a drink and then ate was similarly a rejection, but her amicable compliance came easily enough, simply because it was what he wanted.

The invitation to come up here had meant nothing, then, and it had been unreasonable of her to hope that it might. What could he possibly see in her when she had been so stupidly confused and so angry for most of their short acquaintance? He couldn't think that she was of much interest at all, and even his desire for her had to have been a transitory, intermittent thing, unwanted and probably only occasioned by actual physical contact with her.

And she had promised herself not to be the one to attempt to initiate anything, lest it prove an imposition, and it was becoming very clear that he had no wish for anything more intimate than a sociable evening.

Even when the waiter on special duty had come and cleared away for them after their meal and Lucia had deliberately seated herself on the couch with space for Rob beside her, just in case a miracle should happen and he wanted to get closer to her, he chose to occupy a single chair.

She swallowed as she looked at him, shocked by a pang of longing so intense that it came as a surprise to realise that she hadn't actually cried out with the force of it. With his trousers he was wearing a beautifully made casual shirt, the chalk colour dramatically emphasising the darkness of his skin and hair, and she wanted him very badly.

But there was a certain physical tension about him, to which she had been sensitive all evening, and it seemed as much a denial of her desires as the hardness of his eyes and the taut, almost angry curve of his mouth. He must have sensed something of what she was feeling, and, without bringing it out into the open, this was his way of rejecting her, keeping a distance between them both emotionally and physically.

They continued to talk of netural things, the only remotely personal topic they touched on being the other hotels to which he was planning to give some future attention. One was in the Maldives, and Lucia's face lit up.

'Oh! I lived there too once.' She gave a quick smile at the memory. 'Dugongs are sometimes seen in those waters as well. Maybe you'll meet a mermaid.'

'I don't want a mermaid.' Their eyes collided. 'I want you.'

For several moments Lucia half believed that her imagination had supplied the words, just because she had been longing so intensely for something of the kind.

'Rob. . .?' she faltered uncertainly. 'Really me?'

A slight laugh came from him. 'I didn't mean to say that. I've been trying not to all evening, but the fact that you now accept the situation with Olivier makes the temptation irresistible.'

'What about Madelon?' Lucia asked breathlessly.

'What about her? She's charming, and, like any man, I get a buzz out of being pursued. As she's not the sort of woman who is going to be crushed by failure, I haven't bothered actively discouraging her. But nor have I encouraged her—although I'm sure she'll have led you to believe otherwise, as part of her tactics in what she obviously sees as your friendly rivalry. It's you I want, Lucia.'

A slow, radiant smile transformed her face. It was enough. She knew better than to ask him about Shelagh. She would just have to accept her importance in Rob's life for now, but maybe in time she could make him love her. She would have the advantage of being around, part of his day-to-day existence.

'Then what are you doing sitting over there so far away?' she teased.

A slight frown creased his face. 'It's too soon, really, I know. I shouldn't have told you—'

'Too late! You have!'

With no further need either to hide or suppress her own feelings, she surrendered willingly to desire's sweet insistent tug and was on her feet and moving across to him while he was still sitting there.

Gracefully she leaned over him, placing a quick, loving kiss on his brow before easing herself down so that she was half sitting on his lap. She felt Rob's

tension increase and saw the way his face went taut and
still as she wound her arms about him.

'Are you really thinking properly, Lucia?' he
demanded harshly.

'Feeling,' she corrected him lyrically, before pressing
her lips to the corner of his mouth.

His hands left the arms of the chair, coming up to
hold her a little away from him, and she could see
sparks of some emotion in the smoky depths of his
darkening eyes.

'Are you sure, Lucia?' he prompted urgently. 'Oh,
hell! I know I can't expect you to be absolutely certain
yet—'

'You can!' Lucia contradicted him, the words emerg-
ing in a soft rush.

Her heart felt as if it was expanding to accommodate
its load of love. He was so fair. She sensed that the
question was asked for her sake as well as for his.

A fleeting expression of reluctance crossed his face,
hard and unwilling, and it might have deterred her had
she not been so acutely aware of his lithe body's leaping
reaction to her nearness.

Rob really did want her, therefore he should have
her. And even if he didn't love her yet she could dream
that he might some day, and work at achieving that
prize. It was just so simple when you loved. The loved
one's desires took precedence over all other concerns.

A faint breath of laughter escaped him, banishing
the reluctance.

'I can't decide if you're delightfully uninhibited or
just plain reckless,' he admitted, his fingers beginning
to stir, circling sensuously about her upper arms and
shoulders. 'Either way, you're irresistible—so don't go
changing your mind, because I don't think I can let you
go now, my darling.'

'I won't—you won't have to!' Lucia   asserted

emotionally, thrilling to the endearment and then sighing with pleasure as Rob gathered her in closer to him.

'We've known each other such an incredibly short time when you think about it,' he observed musingly, in between scattering kisses along the line of her jaw. 'But I suppose a certain intimacy was prematurely created and then fostered by the particular circumstances, and that has accelerated everything else... You've told me you're not physically adventurous, but it's obvious that getting close to me is one physical adventure that doesn't give you any qualms.'

'It's the only physical adventure I want to have,' she emphasised candidly, impatient to throw herself into it and shower him with all that she had to give.

'I like that,' Rob was murmuring against her ear.

'Then let's go to bed,' she urged.

'What's the hurry? We've got all night,' he reminded her with indulgent amusement.

Rob's mouth found hers, his kiss leisurely but so thorough and searching too that it seemed as if he reached right down into her soul. Lucia was weak and shaking by the time he ended it, only to have him claim her mouth all over again, swallowing her enraptured gasp, the play of his lips and tongue blatantly erotic now.

A little later, when mutual delight blossomed dramatically into the urgent, driving need for something more intense, they both wanted to hurry, rushing headlong towards the explosion of the senses that awaited them.

When they had moved to his bedroom and undressed, dividing their attention between their own and each other's garments, Rob had pulled back the covers from the low, wide bed and left a light on so that they could both observe the beautiful changes that passion had brought to their bodies.

Lucia's skin was flushed and glistening, her breasts

swollen orbs crowned by the dark jewel-glow of her stiffly erect nipples, and she could not be still, writhing and undulating, in thrall to rapture and fiercely mounting desire.

All this was for Rob—this man whose mind had been so sensitive to her every thought and emotion from the day they had met, and whose body was now proving to be equally perfectly attuned to hers. So why should his heart not be the same some day? He was so magnificent in the grip of his passion, his body hard and vibrant, a film of perspiration giving a gleamingly polished look to his skin.

Or rather, this had been meant for Rob, but he was too complete a man only to take and give nothing. With hands and mouth and body he devoted himself to her pleasure, every touch, each caress, whether lightly skimming or voluptuously lingering, always stoking the ravening fire at the heart of her womanhood.

Lucia gave herself up to sensation, but revelled still more rapturously in what his urgently muttered endearments, broken gasps and violently pounding heart told her she was doing for him. She dedicated her love to his happiness, wildly spendthrift, lavishing it on him in a profligate outpouring of emotion.

When the ferociously aching need impelling them became a clamorous imperative, they moved simultaneously to effect the moment of their union. Bodies met, and joined in a primitively passionate surge of thrusting movement, the eternal miracle of male and female symbiosis proving the design perfect one more time, the woman's enveloping reception as sure and positive as the man's confidently powerful invasion.

To be one with Rob brought a towering joy. Lucia had never felt so sensitive, so receptive to pleasure, and answered voluptuously to his throbbing demand, approaching a shattering crescendo of sensation that originated deep within her, where he was moving so strongly, and spread outwards to engulf her entire being.

One fist drummed against his shoulder, beating a frenzied tattoo that had the same rapid, frantic humming-bird rhythm as her ecstasy's convulsions.

'Rob!' His name came from her in a whispering cry as they shuddered together in the final spasm of mutual release.

Then he was withdrawing from her and Lucia collapsed, sated and still mindless, incapable of moving as she waited for her fluttering pulses to calm and her breathing to slow. After a few seconds Rob moved so that he was lying beside her, one arm curled slackly across her, and she did move then, to accommodate the loose embrace, utterly relaxed and beginning to smile.

The power of thought restored itself after a while, and then she couldn't stop smiling.

'Lucia? You are so. . .' The slow, thoughtful words died away, and he was silent and still for so long that she thought he must have drifted off into sleep, but finally he concluded, 'So generous. And an angel.'

'No angel,' she said, with a quivering sigh of laughter.

'No, perhaps not,' he conceded with lazy humour, after apparently thinking about it for several seconds. 'And you're brave—to be willing to move forward so soon, instead of wasting time looking back.'

Lucia sighed contentedly. Maybe there was a hint in there that he felt a time would come when he could stop looking back to Shelagh. She would have to be patient, though. She mustn't trouble him with the fact of her love yet; it would disturb him, or perhaps make him feel guilty. So there was no point in telling him that she had nothing to look back to and yearn for because her relationship with Thierry had been based on illusion, especially as doing so might give Rob a clue about truth that he wasn't yet ready for.

He would know in time, of course, just as he knew

everything else. But she didn't want him to yet, and she doubted if he would want to know either. The fact that she loved him could mean nothing to him now, and he wasn't a cruel man, so he wouldn't relish having to explain that he didn't want her love, and why.

She must watch her words and be careful not to push him into having to reject her love outright in so many explicit words. It wasn't his fault that her heart had chosen him for her to love, so she had no right to burden him with it.

Once again Lucia made the only commitment that, to her, love had ever seemed to demand. She would do, be and give whatever he wanted her to. It hurt, loving a man who didn't love her, and her intrinsic pride still tended to flinch if she thought too much about that facet of it, but the loving was stronger.

Later in the night they made love again, in the dark now, wrapping each other in tenderness so warm and deep and rich that it brought silent tears before detonating into passion once more.

And one more time, in the very early morning, their energy seeming to feed on its own expenditure, desire rampant and inexorable. Rob's passion was so devouring, the rhythmic strokes of his possession so relentlessly fierce, almost desperate, that it seemed as if he was trying to hold onto the night, to stave off the day.

Consumed by a raging welter of ecstatic sensation and complex emotion, Lucia cried out uncontrollably, her mouth and fingers so frenzied that they had to be leaving marks on his skin.

When it was over, she fell into a sleep so swift and sudden that it was almost a faint, but Rob woke her a while later by brushing the hair back from her face with idly caressing fingers.

'You have to be on duty in the shop soon,' he reminded her when she smiled as she realised that he was already showered and dressed.

'And you?' Just out of sleep, she didn't have her voice under control, and the question came out husky and tender.

Rob was seated on the side of the bed, looking down at her, and she was conscious of something reflective about the way his long fingers circled the curves that gave her face its heart shape.

'I must go. I have to say goodbye to my sister—maybe spend a bit of time with her before going to the airport,' he told her abruptly, taking his hand away as she hitched herself up against the pillows, keeping the top sheet covering her breasts.

Lucia just hid her eyes in time as realisation hit her. Oh, god, how could she have misunderstood him so completely? Last night hadn't been intended as the start of an affair. He had meant it to be exactly what it had been—a night in bed with her. A single night. He didn't want her enough for more.

His other affairs had lasted longer than a night, though, even if they had all ended eventually, according to what Nadine had told her, so maybe he hadn't really wanted her very much at all, and making love to her had just been a way of ensuring that she would be so enslaved that she would leave Thierry alone when he was no longer around to keep an eye on her. He hadn't trusted her when she had told him that she didn't want Thierry back, but he couldn't spare any more time for guarding Nadine's interest.

'Well, I hope you have a safe flight, Rob,' she offered politely, pride coming to her rescue, because she couldn't bear the thought of his guessing how much she had read into their lovemaking.

'So formal? After all we've shared, and especially last night, Lucia?' Rob taunted gently. 'Sweetheart, I'm not sure when I'll be back—'

'Don't bother rushing back on my account,' she interrupted tautly, anguish a twisting sensation in her heart. 'Last night was. . .all I wanted. For comfort, like you said.'

There was a brief silence and then Rob said curtly, 'I don't believe you.'

'Why not? Wasn't it all you wanted?' she retorted innocently, acting desperately.

The back of his fingers nudged at her chin. 'Look at me.'

After a moment spent steeling herself she did so, and he transferred his hand to where her fingers had begun a tense, weaving dance about each other.

'What more do you want?' she asked mockingly. 'I really won't be going after Thierry, Rob.'

'Then anything more I might want becomes irrelevant,' he snapped. 'Thank you, Lucia. I'll be satisfied with that.'

He released her hands with an abruptness that was a rejection, bringing a poignant tightening to her throat.

'Rob. . .'

She still didn't have her act properly together, and the way she whispered his name was very shaky and emotional. His features tautened as he heard.

'Yes, Lucia, I know last night was a mistake!'

'My mistake!'

'So you're regretting it already?' Rob taunted. 'Then there's no point in my hanging around. I must go. Is there anything you need from your room? I can find Madelon on my way out and ask her for you if you like?'

'No, there's nothing—as long as I can make use of your bathroom.' Lucia eyed the dress that she had worn last night, a pool of sumptuous green on the long, low table at the foot of the bed, and her laughter had a betrayingly brittle ring to it. 'It's not as if I'm going to be slipping back to my room in the sort of ball-gown or cocktail dress that would really give us away. Or was public knowledge the object of the exercise?'

The impulsively mocking question brought a blazing anger to Rob's eyes as he stood up. 'You know damned well it wasn't, Lucia,' he snapped furiously.

She had dropped her eyes fleetingly, enraged with herself, but now she raised them again, the look she gave him very clear.

'Yes, I do. It was something much simpler than that. Maybe you should go. Thank you for making me so happy all night.'

It drove the rage away, but the smile he gave her was sardonic.

'No. Thank *you*, Lucia,' he said significantly, and she had an idea that he sighed slightly before straightening his shoulders and adding easily, 'I suppose I may see you again, if you're still around next time I have to visit the island, but, if not, then I hope everything goes well with you, whatever you choose to do—and remember to stay free to choose. Goodbye.'

Ask me to go with you!

The thought was so full of anguished longing, almost willing him to ask, that for a moment she thought she might have begged aloud, but Rob's face didn't change.

He didn't ask her, of course, and Lucia watched him turn and walk away out of the bedroom, through the open door leading to the suite's living area. She saw him pause and pick up a single small piece of luggage which he must have taken through while she had still been sleeping. Then he moved out of her line of vision and she heard the suite's outer door being opened and then firmly closed a few seconds later, the sound somehow as final as a full stop.

With a shuddering sigh, she put her hands over her face and wondered what she was going to do with the rest of her life.

CHAPTER TEN

A SPRING tide was due the weekend before Christmas and its ebb completely uncovered the reef late on the Saturday afternoon. Lucia was off duty, and she wrapped herself in a soft, snowy pareo that accentuated her delicate tan and the fair sun-streaks glinting in her hair, and walked out to the rocks on bare feet.

She had rarely sought solitude in her life and she liked it even less now, tending to seek the company of such friends as Hassan, Madelon and Chester in her leisure hours, as an aid to keeping thought and consequent pain at bay. But she had been among people for most of the day—escorting a minibus tour on a circuit of the island, with a picnic lunch at Chomoni Beach— and the colourful riches of the reef had always fascinated her, as long as she didn't have to dive to inspect them.

She was thinking about her friends as she wandered along just inside the reef. Hassan had been one for many years, but Madelon and Chester were new. She was glad that she had them, especially in this season which was so much a time for sharing with families or lovers—but she wasn't going to start thinking like that again! It made the yearning loneliness too much to bear, and then not even friendship could ease it.

Most of the islanders themselves didn't celebrate Christmas, but the hotel's various restaurants had been booked to capacity for both Christmas Eve and lunch the following day by the non-Islamic sector and such temporary residents as business people and embassy staffs.

The hotel was already sporting an attractive mix of

African and traditional European decorations, waiters were being drilled, chefs were hyper, and both a top cabaret act and a rock group were due to arrive on one of today's flights into Hahaya.

Lucia's mother had written in response to her letter explaining that she and Thierry were no longer getting married and that she was working here until she could afford to leave. She had urged Lucia to come to England in time for Christmas, the nice-sounding man who was soon to become her stepfather having offered to pay her fare.

Lucia had declined without giving the matter very much thought, except to reflect that her refusal would probably ease the mind of the man her mother was marrying. He was obviously generous and tolerant to have offered when the story of how she came to be stranded here must make her seem feckless in the extreme, but he had to have wondered if he was being wise.

She felt little inclination to leave the Comoros at present. She was as comfortable here as anywhere, and even the likelihood of encountering Thierry and Nadine at some stage held no terrors for her. In fact, she had seen nothing of them since Rob had left, and heard nothing either—although Hassan had passed on the local gossip concerning Beth Olivier's latest trip to South Africa: she had bought a townhouse for herself, intent on leaving the couple alone once they were married.

Lucia thought that she might just decide to stay on, especially now that Chester had changed her job yet again, claiming that she was wasted in the hotel shop. She could make a proper career of what she was doing now—

But she wanted more than a career.

She had to stop thinking these things! Resolutely, Lucia went on with what in essence was the non-planning of her life, knowing that she would simply drift into remaining, lacking any personal incentive to motivate her. . .

She would stay here for ever, like some cobwebbed bride in a gothic tale, waiting to see if Rob ever came back, and perpetually reliving their brief relationship, remembering with pain whenever she was somewhere she had once been with him—such as down at the harbour in Moroni and on the beach back there, deserted now that the sun was falling down a green sky towards invisible mainland Africa.

The hotel guests would mostly have repaired to one or other of the happy hours going on in the various bars by now. She ought to join them, wearing a smile and pretending it really was a happy hour.

Lucia started walking back the way she had come, following her extended shadow, the expanse of damp sand that stretched out before her gleaming in the rich lemon light of the setting sun behind her.

Further ahead, the pale sand of the beach proper was dry and powder-fine, no longer brilliant white at this hour but softly gold, becoming rosy, with the stray grain here and there, the myriads sparkling in testimony to what it had once been before time and the ocean had ground it to its present insignificance.

Above the beach, a tall man in a light-coloured shirt and jeans was standing motionless beneath a coconut palm, looking out to sea, or looking at her—

Looking for her?

For the space of a second Lucia imagined that she had conjured him up. She had thought so much and longed so intensely, constantly seeing Rob in her mind's eye, that the force of her frustrated emotions seemed finally to have made him real.

She had faltered momentarily, but now she continued walking with a little upward jerk of her chin. The old pride had tried to reassert itself since Rob's

departure from the island, but it had had nothing to
feed on because she had had nothing to be ashamed
of—save the fact that he didn't love her, and her
stupidity in reading too much into the night they had
spent together.

All the same, she didn't think she wanted him
guessing just how profoundly she had suffered since he
had gone away—more than she had dreamed was
possible.

He was coming to meet her and her heart was racing
in her breast, making her afraid that she might start
hyperventilating, or that her legs would give way.

They met just where the sand became dry, and stood
still, a metre apart. Lucia stared thirstily, drinking in
the sight of him, a clenching sensation manifesting itself
in both heart and loins as she registered that he was
still the same beautiful man she loved, still so vital and
quirkily attractive, still magnetic, still loved and
desired. . .

Bathed in this warm, golden-hued sepia light, the
darkness of his hair and skin had a burnished look, and
she was disturbingly conscious of the deep glow in the
smoke-coloured eyes, under which lay faint brown
smudges similar to those she saw shadowing her own
face every time she looked in a mirror.

'What are you back for?'

The need to fight her feelings made her sound
hostile, and she saw the tension evident in his face
increase as he registered it. She was sorry—but how
were you supposed to meet and greet a former lover,
especially when the great affair had lasted all of a
night? Casually, or with a kiss? What was the etiquette?

'Various things,' he was answering her rather tightly,
'including my sister's wedding. She finally decided to
get married on Christmas Eve, of all times.'

Lucia stared at him blankly for the few seconds it
took her to realise what he was talking about.

'Oh! I'd almost forgotten about that. I hadn't heard,' she confided indifferently.

Rob's eyes had narrowed.

'Why aren't you heartbroken by the news? Been *comforting* yourself again, Lucia? With Hassan Mohammed this time, or have you met someone new?' he taunted softly.

'No, I have not, and why should I be heartbroken?' Lucia lost her temper, and with it, all caution. 'Thierry and Nadine's arrangements are a matter of purely social interest to me, and you might as well know that it's nothing new. You needn't have gone to the lengths you did to stop me going after him after you'd left the island, because I already knew then, that last night, that I didn't love him. I don't think I ever loved him properly, in the way I should have to have been thinking of marrying him.'

'What are you talking about?' Rob demanded.

Her hand chopped furiously at the air. 'I should have known long ago, but I only realised that day I gave him his ring back. Even when I still thought I was marrying him, I wasn't in a hurry—at least, not to marry, only for the side of it which would give me somewhere to belong; I was going to ask him for time before our wedding, so I could try working in one or other of the hotels, because I'd have had to stay home on the estate after we were married.

'I kept. . . After I got back to the island and he was getting engaged to Nadine, there kept being moments when I actually felt almost glad. . .because I was free! I must have wanted to be, so maybe I'd got over wanting to be settled in one place, with a home that isn't rented or on loan. I think it was the life we lived with my dad—always on the move, making new friends and having to leave them behind—that made it seem so important.

'Thierry should have been just my first proper

romance, not all the rest of it—a whole engagement and maybe even marriage. I got too used to the idea; it made me emotionally lazy—him too—and what would I have done if there hadn't been Nadine and I'd realised we were trapped?'

The appeal was angrily agonised, and she stared at him aggressively, but Rob appeared to have relaxed, and his eyes were alight with some strange emotion.

'Don't you think you might have found the courage to tell him and break it off? That's a question, not comforting rhetoric, angel, because I've no easy answers for you, knowing you as I do.'

'And the answer is no, I wouldn't, isn't it?' she challenged bitterly, able to appreciate his honesty. 'Because I'm stupid; I do things, try to be what people want me to be when I love them, and I'd have stayed *fond* of Thierry.'

'So it rests with whether you'd have realised you were damaging him,' Rob suggested. 'I think you might have done in time.'

'Too late, knowing me,' she mocked tautly. 'And I suppose that's another thing you know—that I'm obstinate. I don't like admitting I've been wrong.'

'Which of us does?' Rob paused. 'I seem to have been wrong about a few things—though partly due to some deliberate misleading on your part, my lady, as what you've just told me suggests that you were not, as you claimed, looking for comfort that night we spent together.'

Realising how much her anger had led her into giving away, Lucia flushed.

'Well, whatever my reasons were, at least they weren't as cynical as yours!'

'It seems to me that you haven't a clue what mine were, but forget that for a moment. Would you like to accompany me to this wedding, and see your ex safely off?' Rob was smiling. 'It's expected of me, and entirely appropriate, to attend with a partner.'

'And you haven't arrived with anyone suitable?' she prompted sweetly. 'Why don't you invite Madelon Brouard?'

'No. You.' Rob was inexorable.

'To pretend or for real?' she mocked.

'No pretence is necessary,' he shot back.

'Oh, right,' she agreed tartly. 'So we go out, attend the wedding, share a dinner or two, and, on your last night here, we go to bed again and then you split for however many weeks or months or years. No, thanks, Rob. I don't want to do it again.'

Because she knew now. She had longed for him, for just the sight of him, but the last few seconds had educated her. His absence had been easier. Seeing him intensified a thousandfold the ache that was loving and not having. She couldn't bear it, so it was better not to see him.

'Not even if I love you?' The words were simple, direct and challenging.

'That's not funny!' It was a cry of outrage.

'It wasn't meant to be.'

'Then what—?' Breaking off, Lucia gestured wildly in denial, her face anguished. 'Oh, it's not true! You don't—you can't!'

Rob's eyes had narrowed, and he was scrutinising her intently now.

'Tell me why not,' he invited her silkily.

'How can you?' she appealed hopelessly. 'You went away and left me!'

'What else was I to do when you had just told me you'd had all you wanted of me—a night in my bed for comfort?' Rob responded tautly.

'But you were going anyway, before I said that,' Lucia protested warily.

'But only after I'd secured a promise from you that

you'd wait for me to come back and—court you; or at least let us explore together what was between us,' he emphasised. 'But when you started talking about Olivier, saying you wouldn't be going after him but admitting that you'd only turned to me for comfort, I decided it was pointless. It seemed to me that if you could think of him just then you weren't even beginning to get over him yet.

'I had to go, my darling. I'd already stolen a night with you, long before I meant to. I needed to go for business reasons anyway, but I also had things to examine and decide about myself. Most importantly, it was too soon for you, and even if I'd known you'd stopped loving Olivier you'd had a rough time and were still off balance. Whatever you were feeling for me had come too early; you'd have started wondering if you were making a mistake, misleading yourself.

'I had to give you time to be sure, and a chance to try out your freedom and discover if you preferred it to emotional commitment... I know I shouldn't have made love to you before I went, and I never intended to, but—I needed something to take away with me.'

'Maybe you also needed to give me something to hold on to. That's what it would have been if I'd known you...' She had been speaking softly, taking a small step towards him, but she stopped as incredulity reasserted its hold. 'Do you really love me, Rob?'

'So much, Lucia,' he affirmed simply, and sighed. 'I couldn't have stayed away much longer. Even without Nadine's wedding, even without your speech about only having wanted me for comfort—and that hurt like nothing else ever has before—it's about now that I'd have succumbed and returned.'

'Oh, I wish I'd waited for you to explain! When I realised you were leaving I thought one night with me was all you'd wanted, and then it seemed you must have meant it as a way of stopping me trying to get

Thierry back, because I know your other affairs have lasted longer than that. I suppose it was pride making me say what I did. . .

'You know, I didn't need time, Rob.' She had begun to smile. 'I was sure from the moment I realised I loved you.'

She saw his eyes blaze with exultant emotion. As she reached him Rob lifted his hands to the sides of her face and she ran her own compulsively over the muscled length of his arms, reacquainting herself with the feel of him, assuring herself that he was real.

Then they moved closer to each other, and Rob's mouth dropped to hers in a kiss so emotional that Lucia was left shaken but sure, and radiantly happy.

'One thing still disturbs me slightly,' he confided. 'Our different natures, sweetheart. I'm possessive and demanding, and then there's the incredible way you love—so generously, giving yourself so completely.'

'You once told me you liked women who give all of themselves,' she reminded him, bewildered and breathless.

She was still bound to him by the strong arms about her back, and she had tipped back her head, adoring him with her eyes as the deepening amber light turned his strong idiosyncratic features to gleaming bronze.

'And I do—but I don't want sacrifices, Lucia,' he stated decisively. 'It would be so easy, too easy, for me to accept them from you just because it's in your nature to sacrifice where you love. I could demand everything unreasonable of you, and you'd never object, would you?'

'There are no sacrifices in love, Rob,' she said quietly, and he caught his breath, but then sudden doubt assailed her. 'But. . .what about Shelagh? You're still in love with her.'

'I am not; I haven't been for years, and even when I was it was a pale, tame thing beside the way I love you.

Lucia, being apart hasn't changed anything for you? Hasn't made you think you'd prefer to live without me?' he prompted.

Then he saw what was in her eyes, and smiled. 'All right. I've done a lot of thinking. I know I can't give you up, but I will try not to let my possessiveness lead me into demanding too much of you. That's how much I love you. I could never be bothered to try and conquer the flaws in my nature for Shelagh, for instance, and it was easy enough to let her go... But I *want* to overcome them for you, and I *will* try. You must decide what you want to do—train for personnel work or go in for some other kind of hotel work—and we'll try to find a way to fit ourselves and my travelling around it.'

'No, anything I do has to fit around *us*,' she decreed with tender confidence. 'Do you want to marry me, Rob?'

'Yes!' She saw his eyes blaze positively and tightened her hold on him. 'But I don't want it to mean your giving up whatever you want to do. We'll have to work something out.'

'Why, can't you affort to support a wife?' Lucia enquired mischievously, and as he laughed she went on seriously, 'Rob, I just want to be with you. I don't particularly want a career, and especially not if that's all I can have, or if it means being separated from you. I haven't got a vocation of any sort. I just like mixing with people, and we can compromise there. Love is about compromise, not sacrifices.

'You see, Chester Watson has changed my job again. I'm not in the shop any more; I'm part of the hospitality staff—a sort of hostess and guide. I'm still escorting tours as well. I know it would be a bit nepotistic, but I could do the same on a sort of roving basis, wherever you had to be, couldn't I? I've lived on all the islands where you have hotels, so I know them—and I am good! You can ask Chester.'

'I don't need to.' Lucia felt Rob's relief, and understood just how much he had been prepared to do for her. 'But, in fact, I'm seriously thinking of basing myself more or less permanently in Mauritius, as it has probably the best infrastructure with regard to communications, transport, financial transactions and the like, and I'd only travel briefly, as and when necessary.'

'I love Mauritius! There we are, then!' she exclaimed delightedly, and kissed his throat lovingly. 'And never talk about my making sacrifices again when you were willing to make such a one for me, my darling. But I'll probably only work a year or two. I'm not ready yet, but you do want a family, don't you?'

'Absolutely.' Rob had begun to laugh. 'You can let me know when you're ready.'

'Oh, I won't have to; you'll know anyway,' she predicted lightly, but then her mouth took on a rueful shape. 'Rob, I'm never going to be much of a mystery to you, am I?'

He stirred, his hands moving to caress the smooth curves of her bare shoulders, and a tremor ran through her.

'But you are,' he told her. 'Look how much I've had wrong about you! And it's a complete mystery to me how anyone so proud and sensitive can be so generously willing to give so much of herself, and to give up so much to those she loves. I'm going to have to be so careful not to take advantage of that willingness, and I want you to tell me if I ever seem to be moving in that direction.'

'I will,' she promised, realising that it was vitally important to him. 'But you do know almost everything about me, don't you? And some of it is terrible—

'Oh, Rob! How can you love me when you know all my faults?'

Disbelief had flared again, making her sound panicky and vulnerable.

'If they're faults, they're such lovely ones.' He put his arms round her again, cradling her against him. 'Generosity, consideration, sensitivity. . . I do love you, Lucia. I'm always going to.'

'I like it,' she realised with surprise. 'You know it all and you still love me! I used to hate the way you understood everything about me.'

'I know.' He was drily reminiscent.

'But then I went from resenting it to relying on it,' she confessed. 'That's why. . .Rob, I felt so—so abandoned, when you. . .you didn't really want to know, to comfort me, when I was crying like a fool that day I gave Thierry his ring back.'

'Oh, Lucia, I couldn't. I was too disappointed. You were letting go, giving him up, but you weren't saying the words I wanted to hear, that you no longer loved him, and I assumed you were crying for him!'

'I should have said something,' she realised, ashamed. 'I know I didn't then, but there were other things I didn't know yet, and even when I knew I loved you I didn't think *you'd* want to know, and telling you what I'd realised about Thierry might have made you guess.'

'I wish I had!' Rob gave her a quick smile and continued reminiscently, 'Additionally, by then I'd stopped wanting to anger and alienate you. I didn't want to give you more cause to resent me than you already had, and I was sure that once you'd recovered you would do so, because I'd seen you like that, with your defences down. I loved you by then. I can't claim to have consciously loved you instantly, but I was attracted to you from the beginnning.'

'Me too, to you,' Lucia inserted joyously. 'The first moment I saw you—and I still thought I was engaged to Thierry then!—I had to make myself stop looking. Then you came over and. . .'

'And gave you cause to resent me by being the messenger,' Rob accepted regretfully. 'I did understand a lot of you, almost at once, and I admired you—even when I was still telling myself I didn't like women like you. You were so courageous, with your brave smile whenever you knew you were on show. . .

'I think loving you probably started when I saw you with your hand on Thierry Olivier's shoulder and I suddenly felt so possessive; I didn't want you touching another man because you should have been mine.

'Without even knowing why I was doing it at first, I started being a little bit more careful about the things I said to you. You were humiliated by what he'd done, and by my knowing, and I didn't want you to be; I didn't want to alienate you further when I knew how much you already resented me for having been the messenger and having witnessed what the message did to you. . . I didn't want to cause you any more distress.'

'You never will again.' Lucia paused as she remembered something. 'Rob, you once said you'd never be able to be sure with me if I was on the rebound from Thierry, but you must know by now that it's not that?'

'I knew as soon as I'd said it that I was wrong.' Rob's hands were on the move again, stroking over her back, warming her through the thin cotton of her pareo. 'I knew then, and having to accept what you said about wanting comfort went completely against my fundamental sense of you.'

Lucia's hands were caressing the centre of his back as she looked up into his face, which was very dark now that the evening light had faded to a coppery dusk.

'We've given each other a difficult time, haven't we?' she prompted, and saw him smile.

'So maybe we deserve each other?' Rob quipped tenderly.

'Yes, I think we do,' Lucia agreed happily, and no more was said for a while as they proceeded to prove that they truly did.

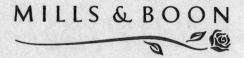

MILLS & BOON

Next Month's Romances

Each month you can choose from a wide variety of romance with Mills & Boon. Below are the new titles to look out for next month.

MISCHIEF AND MARRIAGE	Emma Darcy
DESERT MISTRESS	Helen Bianchin
RECKLESS CONDUCT	Susan Napier
RAUL'S REVENGE	Jacqueline Baird
DECEIVED	Sara Craven
DREAM WEDDING	Helen Brooks
THE DUKE'S WIFE	Stephanie Howard
PLAYBOY LOVER	Lindsay Armstrong
SCARLET LADY	Sara Wood
THE BEST MAN	Shannon Waverly
AN INCONVENIENT HUSBAND	Karen van der Zee
WYOMING WEDDING	Barbara McMahon
SOMETHING OLD, SOMETHING NEW	
	Catherine Leigh
TIES THAT BLIND	Leigh Michaels
BEGUILED AND BEDAZZLED	Victoria Gordon
SMOKE WITHOUT FIRE	Joanna Neil

Delicious Dishes

Would you like to win a year's supply of simply irresistible romances? Well, you can and they're FREE! Simply match the dish to its country of origin and send your answers to us by 31st December 1996. The first 5 correct entries picked after the closing date will win a year's supply of Temptation novels (four books every month—worth over £100). What could be easier?

A	LASAGNE		GERMANY
B	KORMA		GREECE
C	SUSHI		FRANCE
D	BACLAVA		ENGLAND
E	PAELLA		MEXICO
F	HAGGIS		INDIA
G	SHEPHERD'S PIE		SPAIN
H	COQ AU VIN		SCOTLAND
I	SAUERKRAUT		JAPAN
J	TACOS		ITALY

Please turn over for details of how to enter ☞

How to enter

Listed in the left hand column overleaf are the names of ten delicious dishes and in the right hand column the country of origin of each dish. All you have to do is match each dish to the correct country and place the corresponding letter in the box provided.

When you have matched all the dishes to the countries, don't forget to fill in your name and address in the space provided and pop this page into an envelope (you don't need a stamp) and post it today! Hurry—competition ends 31st December 1996.

Mills & Boon Delicious Dishes
FREEPOST
Croydon
Surrey
CR9 3WZ

Are you a Reader Service Subscriber? Yes ❑   No ❑

Ms/Mrs/Miss/Mr _____

Address _____

_____

_____ Postcode _____

One application per household.

You may be mailed with other offers from other reputable companies as a result of this application. If you would prefer not to receive such offers, please tick box.   ❑

C396
F